William Gorman Wills

Drawing Room Dramas

William Gorman Wills

Drawing Room Dramas

ISBN/EAN: 9783337342333

Printed in Europe, USA, Canada, Australia, Japan

Cover: Foto ©Andreas Hilbeck / pixelio.de

More available books at **www.hansebooks.com**

DRAWING ROOM DRAMAS.

BY

WILLIAM GORMAN WILLS,

Author of " Charles I." &c.

AND THE

HON^{BLE.} MRS. GREENE.

WILLIAM BLACKWOOD & SONS,

EDINBURGH AND LONDON.

MDCCCLXXIII.

M

CONTENTS.

—◆—

LURALIE, THE WATER SPRITE.

IN TWO ACTS.

BY

W. G. WILLS, Esq.

Author of "King Charles the First," "The Man o' Airlie,"
"Hinco," "Medea."

DRAMATIS PERSONÆ.

THE GERMAN BARON.
THE FRAU (*his wife*).
JOHANNA (*their daughter*).
ZŒLINE (*her lover*).
WILHELM (*lover of Elspeth*).

ELSPETH (*Johanna's maid*).
THE RHINE KING.
GOBBET (*a Sprite*).
WIZARD.
MERMAIDS.

LURALIE (*the Water Sprite, and also Johanna's rival*).

DRESS.

BARON.—Blue woollen nightcap; long dressing-gown, very much stuffed out; large worsted slippers; swollen gouty feet; white wig and beard; and a walking-stick.

FRAU.—High German cap; long earrings; white lawn handkerchief over a velvet bodice; green quilted petticoat; high-heeled boots.

JOHANNA.—Ruby velvet dress, with a long train, body cut square; gold necklace, bracelets, &c.; hair drawn off the face over puffs, and prettily dressed with white ostrich feathers; fan; white boots, with rosettes to match the dress.

ZOELINE.—Black velvet suit, slashed with white; lace ruffles; silk stockings; shoes with buckles.

LURALIE.—Long flowing dress of white muslin, looped up on the shoulders with crystal pendants, and a girdle of the same round her waist (the drops from a chandelier can be used for this purpose); a coral wreath in her hair, which falls down over her shoulders; a wand in her hand, with a water-lily at the end of it.

WILHELM.—Large linen collar, and necktie with long ends; green swallow-tail coat, with brass buttons; yellow waistcoat, and white trousers.

ELSPETH.—Thick white muslin chemisette and long sleeves; Swiss body, of black silk or velvet; blue skirt, rather short; white muslin cap and apron, and sandalled shoes.

THE RHINE KING.—Very long white hair and beard; face thickly powdered; completely enveloped in a long white sheet.

GOBBET.—Encased in green glazed calico, face and all, with holes cut for mouth and eyes. He wears a long tail, also covered with green calico.

WIZARD.—Spectacles and beard; long black robe, lined with scarlet; and pointed shoes.

MERMAIDS dressed in white muslin; their hair hanging down; wearing wreaths of coral or water-lilies.

ZOELINE, when he appears after he uses the ointment, must wear a mask painted to represent scales, and also a scaly covering on his hands.

The songs and choruses may be sung, if necessary, behind the scenes; or if this be not feasible, spoken by the children.

LURALIE, THE WATER SPRITE.

ACT I.

SCENE I.—WIZARD *alone in his room.*

WIZARD.

For eighty years I studied magic lore ;
I slaved in patience eighty years and more
To friendless age, from manhood bold and lusty,
Mid moths and mildew, skulls, and volumes musty.
Here do I live, in gloomy study housed,
A poor disciple of old Doctor Faust.
One night I watched o'er human joy and dole,
From the small skylight of my glory hole :
The woods and silver-sheeted Rhine I viewed,
When from his bosom rose the scaly brood
Of Sprites and Mermen, o'er the water popping,
And, in fantastic gambols, springing, flopping,
Diving, and splashing, till tormented Rhine
With foam and phosphorus seemed to splash and shine ;
Then one white figure, all in white arrayed,
Swam right ashore, and for the forest made.
I marked her well, as was a wizard's duty.
She was a nymph of most surpassing beauty.
Even I could feel a soft emotion rise

At her gold clouds of hair and dreamy eyes.
Onward she went, like one that walked in slumber;
I breathed a spell, and named a magic number:
Some potent counter charm seemed to prevail,
For on she went—tho' moved and deadly pale.
The Baron's Castle, then, I saw her enter;
She'll make sad mischief, if I can't prevent her.
Old Faust, when powers of evil used to cross him,
Would open at the sign of "Macrocosm;"
Now, following his illustrious example,
I'll view the magic page, mouldy and ample.

                                     [Opens the book.

A sound of rushing water meets my ear.
Ho! scaly spirit, at my call appear!

             *[*GOBBET, *a green Sprite, jumps out of the book.*

GOBBET.

I come, good master. Ho! I come like winkin'.

WIZARD.

Most promptly done, my stern command now drink in.
Some time ago, upon a moonlight night,
Entered yon Castle, a fair Water Sprite.
My wonted skill was useless, I confess,
And soon, no doubt, she made a precious mess.

GOBBET.

Aye, aye, good sir; you mulled the business nicely.

WIZARD.

Long time I knew not what to say precisely.
She has inveigled from his late affection
The Fraulein's lover, of immense connection;
She loves the Sprite, and leaves the Baron's daughter,
And soon, I fear, she'll lure him to the water.

GOBBET.

A pretty story! What's your will, good master?

WIZARD.

Haste to the Castle—counteract disaster.
Promptly upon the Water Sprite attend;
But with sly acts the family befriend.

[GOBBET *bows grotesquely and exit.*

SCENE II.—*The old BARON alone in his study.*

BARON.

I'm in the grumps—but why, I cannot tell—
I'm very ill—I'm seriously unwell;
Though for domestic bliss by nature fitted,
Smacked by my wife, and by my daughter twitted.
But this new comer most provokes my gall;
This madcap stranger—who is she at all?
Some say it was at night—some say at noon
She just dropt in, as though dropt from the moon.
She takes her fling, and nothing is debarr'd her;
She rules the roast, and revels in the larder.
With choicest tit-bits keeps her wolfish maw full,
For 'twixt ourselves her appetite is awful;
She chokes my pipe, and laughs at my lumbago,
And rules the Frau, that notable virago!

[FRAU *sings within.*

Hush! 'tis my wife, as grim as an inquisitor!
What saith the proverb, touching the Old Visitor?
Oh! that some opening trap-door would engulph her!
Here comes the old one!—what a smell of sulphur!

Enter FRAU.

FRAU.

[*Aside.*]   I'll try the civil dodge—though scold I ought.
[*Aloud.*]   Well Baron, dear, a penny for your thought.

BARON.

It was not worth so much—I thought of you.

FRAU.

Your answer is amusing, and quite new.
Just now we can't afford to be so funny ;
Pray think about your daughter and your money.

BARON.

My daughter and my ducats—stale old song.

FRAU.

Baron !

BARON.

    Well, go-ahead ! but don't be long.
Poor love-sick daughter ; is she very bad ?

FRAU.

Man ! do you mean to drive me dancing mad ?
All our misfortunes give you little pain,
Caused, every one, by your old fuddled brain.
That most outrageous minx again has crost
Our daughter's marriage prospects—all is lost !
Our wealthy suitor, poor Johanna jilts,
And with that vixen flirts, and talks on stilts,
And skips attendance on her, like a lacquey.
What ! not a symptom of surprise ?

BARON.

         Oh ! Cracky !

FRAU.

I'm in a fury!

BARON.

Take it easy, Frau

FRAU.

Baron, I'll pull your nose, sir!

BARON.

Bow—wow—wow!

FRAU.

I can't believe my ears—whom bark you at?

BARON.

At you, my love!

FRAU.

Take that—and that—and that.

[*Exit* FRAU, *after boxing* BARON's *ears.*

BARON (*alone*).

My bark was vastly better than her bite;
If what she says is true, 'twill serve her right.
I'm always bilious after such a fray—
I'll go to sleep—and not awake to-day.

[*Sings.*

Nothing for your gouty toper,
Safe from noisy interloper,
Like a long refreshing sopor,
   That's the Latin for a doze.
Oh! how cheery when we're weary,
Blandly healing ruffled feeling.

When he's fast asleep and snoring,
Pain and crusty wife ignoring,
Never groaning—never roaring,
  Oh! how glorious is a doze.
Oh! how cheery—when we're weary—
Blandly—healing—ruff—

                        [Sleeps, and snores.

Thunder and lightning. Enter RHINE KING.

BARON (*starting up*).

Ho! all hands to the pump.   Save—Oh! I'm sunk.
I'm either half-seas over—or I'm drunk!
Ho! buckets—brandy—bladders—anything!

RHINE KING.

Behold his Majesty the great Rhine King.
Bid us all hail!

BARON.

        Hallo!   All hail and thunder!
Who's this old water-spout, I greatly wonder?

RHINE KING.

I raised but now above the reedy Rhine
My watery stature, where for ages nine
I held *mild reign*—o'er regions soft and pleasant.

BARON.

Mild rain! my friend, you're raining hard at present.
Have you a chance of clearing? for, by Nemesis!
If you don't clear, I'll quickly clear the premises.

RHINE KING.

Peace, dotard, or I'll founder you with water.
I come to pay a visit to my daughter;
Where does she hold her state?

BARON.

　　　　　　　　　Oh, goodness knows !
Don't you cascade upon my gouty toes.

RHINE KING.

About a month ago, or near that period,
My daughter left my halls, a green-haired Neriad,
And on a moonlight night your Castle sought.
Dost thou remember ?

BARON.

　　　Well, I think I ought.

RHINE KING.

So be it !　How is my daughter thriving ?
How didst thou entertain her on arriving ?

BARON.

She helped herself to everything.

RHINE KING.

　　　　　　　So best.
Nought is too good for such a noble guest.
Go fetch her : bid her wait on no protences.

BARON.

My good fellow, are you in your senses ?
Before I'd leave my chair to fetch your daughter,
I'd see you on the fire and changed to boiling water.

RHINE KING (_furious_).

Insulted to my beard !　But thou shalt quake—dog !
I'll change thy lands and castle to a shake-bog ;

Thy halls shall lodge the loathsome bat and vile owl,
Thyself and Frau shall fly away like wild fowl.
Insulted to my beard so long and hoary !
Vanish *instanter* to a lower story.

BARON *sinks (or drawn aside on his chair.)*   *Enter* LURALIE, *attended by*
GOBBET.

LURALIE.

Of common propriety have you no feeling?
You sent the old Baron right down through my ceiling.
I don't like your beard, nor your great glassy eyes,
And this visit has given me less joy than surprise.

GOBBET.

We're quite happy without you, and not the least lonely.

RHINE KING.

Peace, sea-pig ; I'm speaking to Luralie only.
My crystal fountain, Luralie, thou art :
To see thee lifts the cockles of my heart.
Come back, come back, my Luralie, unto thy home of water,
My halls are sad and lone to me, my daughter, oh, my daughter !
Come back—come back !

LURALIE.

No, thank you, sir.

RHINE KING.

Come back, ma'am.

LURALIE.

Stay I'd rather.

RHINE KING.

Ye thunders, what a dreadful shame !
The girl disowns her father !

LURALIE.

I will not return, were you ever so fluent.

RHINE KING.

Thou art not in earnest, my dear little truant.

GOBBET.

Oh, yes ! quite in earnest, old gentleman.

RHINE KING.

S'blud !

If you speak one word more, I'll dissolve you to mud.
[*To Luralie.*]   Canst thou leave thy old father alone to his sorrow ?

LURALIE.

Oh, yes! you may coax me to-day and to-morrow.

RHINE KING.

Undutiful girl, 'tis thy father who calls :
He longs for thy voice in his desolate halls ;
Each tide that returns his affection grows stronger.

LURALIE.

A very good reason to wait a while longer.

RHINE KING.

Unnatural daughter, my feelings I stifle :
I give thee one month more to wanton and trifle.
Till my sixtieth tide hath returned to the sea,
And the sign of the Fishes reflected shall be
On the blue-water roof of my palace below—
Till then, thou hast power to remain, or to go.

LURALIE.

And how is my pet, the large river trout ?

RHINE KING.

Disconsolately he is swimming about.

LURALIE.

I hope you take care of my great sea-shell.

RHINE KING.

It is safe.

LURALIE.

And my pale river sisters ?

RHINE KING.

                     Are well.
They wait for you here ; you shall see them to-night,
In their fillets of rushes and garments of white.
With a wave of my wand I'll disclose in a jiffy,
Earth's loveliest river, excepting the Liffey.

    [Scene opens: beautiful tableau of Rhine and Nymphs.

There's a mirror that's fit for the stars and the moon.
Come, girls, to old Rhine a sweet madrigal tune.

SONG—NYMPH CHORUS.

Joyfully carol we, joyfully carol we—
   While Father Rhine rolls blithely along.
Merrily let it be—merrily let it be :
   Light as his wave be our song.

RHINE KING.

Hush ! Do you dare to disturb the gravity
Of the stern old Rhine with levity,
Ruffling his serene longevity ? Daughter, chant it solemnly.

NYMPH CHORUS.

Solemnly—solemnly, mighty one, we chant it,
Mournfully let it be, magic tones incanted,
With thy hoary age condoling, turret crowned King for centuries
    rolling,
Moaning wide, thy plaintive tide, swelleth our chorus solemnly.

KING.

Farewell, my daughter, till the fatal day ;
But pause not, when thy carriage stops the way.

[Exit all.

SCENE III.—A Room in the Castle. LURALIE seated.

Enter FRAU and JOHANNA.

JOHANNA.

Oh, mother, speak to her, you must implore her :
Just lay my melancholy case before her ;
Tell her I know that half in sport 'tis done,
But say she's killing me, and all for fun.
Ask her the cause of the ill-will she bears me,
Say I will try to love her, if she spares me.

FRAU.

You know, my dear, it never was my weakness
To stoop to wrongs, or insolence, with meekness.
The fact, indeed, your silly father knows,
That creature has bewitched me, I suppose :
My tongue to do its duty quite refuses,
And at my fingers' ends my courage oozes.

LURALIE (getting up).

What want you, Frau ? Pray hasten, we're engaged.

FRAU.

Is she an Empress ? Oh, I am enraged !
Ma'am, I must say your actions are most strange :
We hope your line of conduct you will change !
[*Aside.*]   I cannot scold her, there's no use in trying.

LURALIE.

I see you think me far too self-denying,
But at your kind request, so urgent really,
I shall indulge myself somewhat more freely.

FRAU.

I wish I could—

LURALIE.

Express for me your kindness.

JOHANNA.

Those who won't see, how hopeless is their blindness.

FRAU.

Don't you intend to take a nice excursion ?
We should contribute much to your diversion.
You are not looking well.   I wish you would ;
'Twould brace your nerves, and do a deal of good.
Far up the Rhine, by steam and favouring tide.
Pray do ; we'll furnish you with Wier's Guide.

LURALIE.

Good Frau, you never could get on without me ;
I've such engaging little ways about me.
You dear old thing, that turban is so tasty—
Now just run down, and mind the ven'son pasty.
Come, such a bustling housewife I would make you.

FRAU.

Am I the mistress here ?   Oh, sorrow take you.

[*Exit* FRAU.

LURALIE (*to Johanna.*)

Well, Fraulein dear, I thought you would escort her.

JOHANNA.

If you had any heart, you'd give me quarter.
Dear Luralie, to my petition hearken,
And don't my little gleam of sunshine darken—
Don't treat a poor young creature in this fashion ;
But give me back my lover in compassion.

LURALIE.

Pray what's all this about ? you must be raving.
Is it my gay young bridegroom you are craving
You take him for a puppet ; can I make you
A present of a youth, if he won't take you ?

JOHANNA.

Don't be too sure, though little you suspect,
You may find out my hopes are not all wrecked.

LURALIE.

Soft then ! We'll try. Your Zoeline you'll find
Somewhere about the study window blind :
Make up to him ; I'll hie to the plantation,
While you engage in desperate flirtation.
But in the midst, when you shall be most tragic,
I'll softly sing an air of sweetest magic ;
I lay you any wager that you'd wish
He'll leave you lonely, as a stranded fish.

JOHANNA.

Presumptuous girl ! I lay you two to one,
Though not to betting given.

LURALIE.

Fair Fraulein, done !

[*They shake hands.*

JOHANNA.

Then I defy you, you may do your best.
I'll put my fortune to a final test.

[*Excunt* L. *and* R.

Enter FRAU *and* ZOELINE *different ways.*

FRAU.

Good morning, sir.

ZOELINE.

Good Frau, I give you greeting.

FRAU.

Young gentleman, I long have sought this meeting.
Why don't you blush for shame ?

ZOELINE.

Good Frau, in sooth,
I have not blushed, I fear, since tender youth.
You should be grateful; I have done my best
To do the honours to your beauteous guest.

FRAU.

How kind you are !

ZOELINE.

The favour do not mention.

FRAU.

How dare you pay that bold-faced thing attention
In my own house—under my very nose?

ZOELINE.

Well, under what's *as red*—under the rose.

FRAU.

Insolent puppy!

ZOELINE.

Frau, I am not deaf,
Your voice has reached a superhuman clef.
Here comes your daughter, at the row alarmed.

FRAU.

You'll see me soon again.

ZOELINE.

I shall be charmed.

[*Enter* JOHANNA *and* ELSPETH.

The click-clack of that tongue is past enduring.
Oh, there's one voice so sweet and soul-alluring!

JOHANNA.

Dear Zoeline, I'm glad we've met again,
We havn't had a chat I don't know when.
Do you still care for me?

ZOELINE.

Yes, dear, you're right.
[*Aside.*]   I vow her walk is quite ungraceful! quite.

C

JOHANNA.

For months I've been so very sad and lonely,
A heart-disease, and you're the doctor only.

ZOELINE.

Yes, Luralie.

JOHANNA.

My name's Johanna, sir!
I wish you would not think so much of her.

ZOELINE.

Dearest Johanna! justly am I blamed.

JOHANNA.

If folks say true, you ought to be ashamed.
What do you see in that fresh-water shark?

ZOELINE.

Well, now, there is not much in that remark.
My Luralie some pretty speech had turned.

ELSPETH.

My mistress speaks. Where were your manners learned?

ZOELINE.

In looks they cannot be compared a minute,
A gay young nightingale, and poor green linnet.

ELSPETH.

My mistress speaks to you. Come, Master Dapper,
No matter who's your *duck*, I'm not your *flapper*.

ZOELINE.

Pardon, Johanna, pardon this abstraction.

JOHANNA.

Your meditations must have much attraction.
You were not so abstracted, sir, before.
I fear you think my company a bore.

ZOELINE.

Oh, not the least.

[*A low voice is heard singing outside.*
But stay—I beg your pardon—
Don't you hear someone singing in the garden?
I have a small appointment for a while.
[*Aside.*]   Ah! she's without my charmer's brilliant smile.

JOHANNA.

Meanwhile I'll go and sit alone and cry.

ZOELINE.

Aye, do—I mean—I'll see you by and by.
[*Exit* ZOELINE.

JOHANNA.

'Tis hard a girl should break her heart at twenty.
Have you no comfort, Elspeth?

ELSPETH.

Madam, plenty.
He is a puppy, impudent, and snobbish.
How feel you, mistress dear?

JOHANNA.

Pretty bobbish.

ELSPETH.

Don't take on so; how pitiful you talk.
If I'd my will, Miss Luralie should walk.

c 2

I'd rather play the poor fool in the middle,
Than in my father's house play second fiddle.
To call *her* pretty : 'tis a public scandal ;
Why, ma'am, to you she couldn't hold a candle.

JOHANNA.

Why, yes, I *must* confess her eyes are fishy.

ELSPETH.

And her complexion, oh ! so washy-wishy.

Enter LURALIE.

LURALIE.

My pretty Jezebel, what's that you said ?

JOHANNA.

Come, Elspeth, not a word ; we'll cut her dead.

LURALIE.

So sits the wind, how angrily you mutter,
You must have quarrelled with your bread and butter.
On such a lovely day, why look so cloudy ?
Has Frau Mamma been scolding,—the old dowdy ?
Come, Fraulein, here's my hand—forget all wrongs.

ELSPETH.

We wouldn't touch it with a pair of tongs.

JOHANNA.

Oh, Elspeth, don't ;—I bear her no ill-will,
Though you have ruined all my prospects,—still.

[*She shakes hands with* LURALIE.

LURALIE.

Pray, Fraulein, can I help my own attraction?
Why these reproaches?   Can't you take an action?
Some damages you might recover from us,
If you make out a case of breach of promise.
But don't blame *me*—what mischief have *I* done?
You tried to win him,—swimmingly *I* won.
To view it in a piscatorial light,
I angled for him, and he took the bite.
Safe in my meshes lies your brave knight-errant,
While your slack lines are drifting in the current.

[*Sings to the air of "Gin a body meet a body."*

You have lost a gallant lover :
   Wooing me he came.
If I have not chid the rover,
   Am I, ma'am, to blame?

If I bad him welcome only,
   In a pretty song,
When he found me sad and lonely,
   Am I in the wrong?

If I took his hand and mildly
   Bade him not despair,
When he vowed he loved me wildly ;
   Call you this unfair?
                  You have lost, &c. &c.

JOHANNA *sings.*

When you came stealing hope from my heart,
Have I e'er blamed or bid you depart?
When your cold hatred, smiling at face,
Stung this poor heart in trustful embrace,

Who was to blame?   Yes, who was to blame?
Who was the serpent that smilingly came?
Who was to blame?   Yes, who was to blame?
For this stung heart, who's to blame?

When the poor lapwing, flying alone,
Pineth to find her nestlings are gone;
Was the rude hand that wantonly came
Stealing her darlings—was it to blame?
Thus you're to blame,—yes, thus you're to blame;
Yours was the rude hand that wantonly came.
Thus you're to blame; thus you're to blame;
For this robbed heart you're to blame.

                 [*Exeunt* L. *and* R.

SCENE IV.—*The outside of the Castle;* WILHELM *serenading with a fiddle.*

WILHELM.

This is her window.   All are still as mice.
How beautiful is Elspeth—yea, how nice!
And, oh! her dimples, when they slyly come,
Dear heart, they are enough to strike one dumb.
In our short petticoats we were attached,
And once I blubbered when her nose was scratched.
I gave her all my gingerbread and candy,
And one small lock of hair, so nice and sandy;
But now she's been admired, and gone to service,
She laughs at me, and makes me very nervous.
In music, now, I'll tenderly upbraid her,
And if my nerves permit I'll serenade her.
This fiddle once, I'm told, I fingered neatly,
And it discourses music—very sweetly.

[WILHELM *sings ; air, "Summer Night"* (*Don Pasquale.*)

Awake, my dear, I'm fiddling and shivering here ;
   And fiddling and shivering here.
Awake, my dear, and at the top window appear !

                [*Window opens ;* BARON's *head appears.*

Oh, dear ! Oh, dear !—

                       [WILHELM *hides.*

BARON.

Bless me ! I've always heard the place was haunted !
Such frightful howling—not that I am daunted.

                     [*Comes out on the stage.*

Some shocking stories I can recollect.
'Tis right we should be very circumspect ;
No doubt strange characters are now about,
Such as my bumptious friend, Old Water-spout ;
And when such ugly customers are going,
Who may pop in upon us there's no knowing.
Hush !—hist ! What voice was that ? What sudden shade
Popped out behind me ? Bless me ! Who's afraid ?

               [*Sees* WILHELM *going off.*

Hullo ! you thief ! your swallow-tails I'll riddle.
Here's a nice concert of a cat and fiddle.
Ah ! now I see it all—a pretty frolic.
Bless me ! the fright has given me the colic.
Donner und blitzen ! But he got a fright :
He'll scarcely be in tune again to-night ;
I'll have a drop to warm my good old nose.
Oh, my lumbago ! Oh, my gouty toes !

         [BARON *goes into the house ;* WILHELM *comes back.*

WILHELM.

Alas ! I'm in a tremble. It was frightful ;
And I was singing to her quite delightful !

Perhaps 'twas fancy, only superstition,
That hideous, wrinkled, bloated apparition.
Oh, Elspeth ! what I ventured for your sake !
My gentle fiddle shall once more awake.

> [WILHELM *sings; air,*" *Buy a Broom.*"

I've come here to-night, dear, in pitiful plight, dear,
Through danger and fright, dear, a singing to you.

ELSPETH *appears at the window and sings.*

I'm sick of enduring your vile troubadouring,
You don't look alluring.   Poor sweetheart, adieu !
Good-bye now.

WILHELM.

Don't fly now.

ELSPETH.

Good-bye now.

WILHELM.

Don't fly now.

ELSPETH.

Duet. { The household you'll waken.   Poor sweetheart, adieu.

WILHELM.

Don't leave me forsaken, a singing to you.
Still fiddling I'll keep, dear ; I'll sing you to sleep, dear ;
Till morning does peep, dear, I'll sing and I'll sigh.

ELSPETH.

Your sighs are no use, sir ; you're not worth abuse, sir.
Now, don't be a goose, sir.   Poor sweetheart, good-bye.
Good-bye now.

WILHELM.

Don't fly now.

ELSPETH.

Good-bye now.

WILHELM.

Don't fly now.

ELSPETH.

Duet.
The household you'll waken. Poor sweetheart, adieu.

WILHELM.

Don't leave me forsaken, a singing to you.

[ELSPETH *disappears; the door opens.* WILHELM *rushes into the* BARON'S *arms.*

BARON.

Come, sir, give me up your fiddle, you made such a horrible rout
You've given my wife the night-mare, and aggravated my gout.

Enter FRAU.

FRAU.

Good gracious me! why, Baron, what means this outlandish row?
Come, wretch, give up your fiddle: I dreamed they were killing
the sow.

WILHELM.

I can't give up my fiddle. Oh, pardon, good woman, I beg.

FRAU.

Yourself, young man, and your fiddle we'll certainly lower a peg.

BARON.

Begone, rash youth, forswear these mad night capers:
Take your old fiddle, and take to your scrapers.

FRAU.

And if you can't resist your tuneful failing,
You must reserve your music for the railing.

[*Exeunt* L. *and* R.

Scene V.—*A Room in the Castle. Enter* Johanna *and* Elspeth.

JOHANNA.

Quick ! Father wants his lunch—draw in the table ;
Make all as comfortable as we're able.
Here is his meerschaum ; place his gruel here—
'Tis good for gout.   Oh, hide that jug of beer,
And then, perhaps, he'd like to take a light nap ;
Shake up his pillow—where's his gown and night-cap ?
We'll sit with him, it will prevent me fretting.

ELSPETH.

You'll spoil him, ma'am, you'll ruin him with petting.

JOHANNA.

To please my father, could I do too much ?

ELSPETH.

He comes ! hark to the bumping of his crutch.

Enter Baron.

JOHANNA.

Well, father dear, are you complaining still ?

BARON.

Tut ! child, I'm very cross and very ill—
I'm off my oats.

ELSPETH.

　　　　　This petulance give over ;
You're off your oats because you live in clover.
Here is your luncheon, sir.

JOHANNA.

Elspeth, be quiet!

BARON.

What trash is that? What meagre prison diet?

JOHANNA.

'Tis some nice gruel, father.

BARON.

Throw it out!

JOHANNA.

I only thought 'twas very good for gout.
What would you wish, sir?

BARON.

I intend to lunch
On devil'd kidneys and on brandy punch.
They'd have me waste away on bread and water.

ELSPETH.

Fie! You're a pretty man to have a daughter.

JOHANNA.

Oh! ever thus from childhood was my fate!
I don't know how I earned my father's hate.

BARON (*melting*).

I melt to tears. Poor goose! she looks so mild.
Come here, my eldest-born and only child.

JOHANNA.

Dear Sir! I did my best to make you snug.

BARON.

You did, my offspring. Come, a filial hug.
Bless you, my child, my little nurse you'll be.
Sit on your cross old daddy's gouty knee ;
For though his aggravations are not small,
He's not so bad a fellow after all.

Enter FRAU.

FRAU.

I've caught them at their sentimental chatter.

BARON.

Well, woman, well ! you've caught us, and what matter ?

FRAU.

I am not dreaming of you, old Stupidity.
The time is come, we'll seize it with avidity.
I've caught the gallant and that minx together,
Enjoying quietly the summer weather ;
Walking there quietly, above all dodging,
As if they had a right to board and lodging.
Give me your arm, old man, till you behold her—
She'd feast on us, indeed.

BARON.

       We'll give her the cold shoulder.

     [*He hobbles out on* FRAU'S *arm.*

JOHANNA.

Come, Elspeth, quick ! we'll steal off softly now.

ELSPETH.

I go, although I'd like to see the row.

         [*Exeunt.*

Enter ZOELINE *and* LURALIE, *dogged by* BARON *and* FRAU.

FRAU.

There's impudence !   Come, dear, just turn them out.
Quick ! Baron !—be decisive.

BARON.

Oh my gout!

FRAU.

Why, Baron dear, I think you must be drunk.

BARON.

No, Frau, my darling, only in a funk.

FRAU.

Just have their luggage *rolled* off to the coach.

BARON.

That might be deemed a *truc*-ulent reproach.

FRAU.

My mouth is shut when I should furious be.

BARON.

I wish 'twas lock-jaw, and I had the key.

FRAU.

I really don't know how I was outwitted,
But when 'twas *I* myself her stay permitted,
I can't go back.

BARON.

You ought to be a dab
At going back, like any sour old crab.

FRAU (*patting him on the shoulder*).

Baron ! be at them like a dear old fellow.

BARON.

She's licking me—the cobra di capello.

FRAU.

Be at them ! See, they're looking at us now !

GOBBET (*starting out*).

Harroose, old Baron ; Hi ! Harroose, old Frau !

[GOBBET *hunts out* BARON *and* FRAU.

ZOELINE.

Dear Luralie, thus twine our hands together ;
Water or earth shall have no power to sever
This hand from mine.

LURALIE.

Water !   Art thou in earnest ?
I fear thou'lt waver when the truth thou learnest.
Yet I would question thee.

ZOELINE.

Come, love, begin.

LURALIE.

You're webbed, of course, and have a dorsal fin.

ZOELINE.

Yes—and a little tail that's scarcely grown.

LURALIE.

Well, sir, you swim, of course, like any——

ZOELINE.

Stone !

LURALIE.

Pray can you dive when wind and wave are driving?

ZOELINE.

Out of my depth my tendency is diving,
Though from a child I've lived a dip detesting.

LURALIE.

Ah, Zoeline! do stop this dreadful jesting,
Now, should you wed the Rhine King's beauteous daughter,
How long, perhaps, could you stay under water—
Beneath the lovely Rhine, now, were you in it?

ZOELINE.

Well, let me see—suppose we say a *minute*.

LURALIE.

No longer?

ZOELINE.

Well, I shouldn't mind the soaking.
But I'm peculiarly averse to choking.
What's this? In tears! Your meaning I would construe.

LURALIE.

But I *will* weep! Don't comfort me, you monster.
'Tis little that you care about my wishes,
And won't come down to see the pretty fishes.

[*Sings; air, " Come to my gipsy home."*
Come to my water home, lover of mine—
Down in a sparry cave under the Rhine:
There shall you dream away ages of love,
Lulled by the drowsy waves fathoms above;

White nymphs shall wait on us, gliding around—
Gliding in time to the wave's drowsy sound.
There shall I sing as you slumber the while,
And you shall dream in the light of my smile.
Voices are calling us, spirit-like sound
Softly is weaving enchantments around.
Come to my water home, lover of mine,
Down in a sparry cave under the Rhine.

ZOELINE (*much moved*).

I yield, I go ; these words my soul environ ;
I rush to take the fatal plunge, my Siren ;
The Rhine King beckons us with osier truncheon.
I go—but first I think we'll order luncheon.
Ho ! Gobbet !

GOBBET.

Here, sir.

ZOELINE.

I was near forgetting
We'd want a stimulant before the wetting.

|GOBBET *brings wine.*

ZOELINE.

Here's good old Rhenish, and no flavour finer:
A goblet fill up.

GOBBET.

In a fillup, Mein Herr.

ZOELINE.

Stay, for your mistress first a goblet fill.

LURALIE.

Pure water be it, and about a gill.
To-morrow evening, when the moon is up,
You'll find a magic ring within this cup ;

Then, if you really love me, do not linger,
But place the ring upon your marriage finger,
And hasten to the shore, where rustling sedges
And tiny ripples glance with silver edges ;
Where reeds and osiers in the breeze are swinging,
You'll find me combing my long hair, and singing.
But first,—anoint your body with this ointment ;
'Twill make you water-proof,—keep your appointment.

ZOELINE.

Farewell ! my ardent love at nothing quails.

[*Exit* LURALIE.

GOBBET.

That stuff will make him all break out in scales.

ZOELINE *sings.*

Yes, I believe thee, whate'er may betide me ;
Thy music is round me, its cadence shall guide me ;
I'll sleep, and thy form shall be kneeling beside me,
    My cold hand be clasping in thine.
Thus let me sleep—ah ! how calmly reclining,
As o'er me the stars from thy soft lids keep shining,
For ever, for ever in lonely endeavour
    To lighten the darkness of mine.

END OF ACT I.

D

ACT II.

Scene I.—*A Room in the Castle.* LURALIE *alone.*

LURALIE.

My summer holidays are nearly over :
I've roved enough to love to be a rover ;
But *I have* won him, and before I go
Must suit him to our water home below.
That ointment, deadly to all water vermin,
Will change my lover to a gallant merman,
With webs and scales, and horny, lizard tail,
So curled and green—a lovely coat of mail.
This ugly crisis keeps me in the fidgets.
How will he feel with webs between his digits ?
Will scales and lizard tail appear alarming ?
Will he be shocked at what I think so charming ?
This morning I was mischievous and merry ;
My heart danced lightly, like a trim-built wherry ;
But now a cloud so black, it makes me shiver,
Comes flitting o'er my bosom's sunny river,
As in a magic crystal I can see
Some hurricane approach.   Ah ! woe is me !

Enter WIZARD *disguised as a beggar.*

WIZARD.

I am uncertain how I shall accost her.

LURALIE.

I know you well, you funny old impostor.

WIZARD.

Fair one, mistaken you might chance to be.

LURALIE (*mimicking him*).

Nay, never wag your goatish beard at me.

WIZARD.

Madam, you're merry, but I know you not.
The merest chance has brought me to this spot ;
A poor old beggar, spent with hunger's qualms,
Who likes a joke, but far prefers an alms.

LURALIE.

I see, and so by merest chance you came ;
Perhaps you'd make your exit by the same.

WIZARD.

Then be it so.   On purpose I am here.
It seems thou knowest me;—thou shalt learn to fear.
Would'st thou illude the Wizard's piercing sight ?
At this dread sign unmask thee, Water Sprite !

> [*Waves his wand—throws off his disguise.*

LURALIE.

Dear, picturesque old creature, don't be furious !
Oh, what a lovely beard ! so soft and curious ;
'Twould be such fun in two great rolls to plait it,
A waterfall of beard !—now might I pat it ?

> [*She strokes* WIZARD's *beard.*

WIZARD.

No siren art my settled purpose staggers.

LURALIE.

There is no need, dear sir, of looking daggers.

WIZARD.

Spirit, attend !   Unbending I proceed.

LURALIE.

Are you so stern and pitiless indeed ?

WIZARD.

If I relax my brow at your contrition,
Charge it to pity, not to indecision.
Long hast thou fooled it, all my magic scorning.
Ere you proceed, accept a solemn warning :
If on yon youth thou shalt exert thy malice
To lure him to thy father's fatal palace,
Enchanting him with thy allurements hollow,
I tell thee, nymph, dread punishment shall follow.
'Tis writ within my volume's clasped pages—
Eternal anguish, or a sleep for ages ;
But to induce thee to withdraw thy charms
To thy late home, and to thy father's arms,
The sparry vaulted caves thou shalt behold,
See on yon mists the magic scene unrolled.
            [*Tableau of* LURALIE'S *home.   Solemn music.*
So, fade !—Take care ;—thou'rt warned, howe'er it be.
Adieu—adieu—adieu ! Remember me !
                        [*Exeunt* L. *and* R.

Enter JOHANNA *and* ELSPETH.

JOHANNA.

I'm sick of sighing, broken-hearted nearly.
He surely treats me very cavalierly.
                    [*Hands* ELSPETH *a dagger.*
Just take this dagger ;—To my bosom's centre
Strike home, dear Elspeth, till the daylight enter !

ELSPETH.

The daylight enter !—Mistress, you're insane !
Remember daylight enters through a *pain*.
We'll first kill time, dear mistress, if we can.
Here comes my sweetheart !   Such a funny man.

[*Enter* WILHELM.

You come, young man, as usual in the flurries,
A teazing cur.

JOHANNA.

Oh ! you're the lamb he worries.

WILHELM.

I am offended by such cruel dealings ;
In fact, I'm overpowered with my feelings.
Sweet girl, we'd live together very snugly
If you would have me.

ELSPETH.

Why, you are so ugly !

WILHELM.

I know my face is——

ELSPETH.

Like a buttered muffin.

WILHELM.

I know I am a goose.

[*Sighs audibly*.

ELSPETH.

You seem to be a *puffin*.

WILHELM.

Of a small house I have a lease for life.
Oh, be my husband ; let me be your wife.
Two cows do browse an acre and a half.

ELSPETH.

And of which cow are you the happy calf ?

WILHELM (*to Johanna*).

Do, pretty, sweet young woman, help me if you can.

JOHANNA.

Oh, take him, Elspeth, such a nice young man.
A lovely Roman nose and larking eye,
And I am sure he's nearly six feet high.

WILHELM *sings ; air*, "*Mary Blane.*"

This morning to a barber's shop
   To trim my hair I went ;
And on this handsome suit of clothes
   A lot of money spent.

But now, of all the pride I felt
   In these nankeens, you rob
My wretched heart—I feel as if
   They were not worth a bob.

I'll just go home, and round my neck
   A true love knot I'll tie,
And then I'll climb a lamp-post rung
   And hang until I die.

And some dark night, when you are tripping
   Homeward in the damp,
You'll see my poor long helpless legs
   A dangling from a lamp.

ELSPETH *sings ; air, "Trab, trab."*

Here let this folly end, sir,
　　I told you so before ;
I like you as a friend, sir,
　　But, thank you, nothing more.
Perhaps if you should die, sir,
　　I'd wish you back again,
And may be I might cry, sir ;
　　But you must wait till then.
　　　　　　And may be, &c.

Were I your little mate, sir,
　　When you had time to cool,
You find me out, when late, sir,
　　A shrewish little fool.
If you should like to come, sir,
　　To see me now and then,
I'll always be at home, sir ;
　　But talk no love again.
　　　　　　I'll always, &c.

　　　　　　　　　　　[*Exeunt.*

Enter ZOELINE *with a glass, applying ointment to his face.*

ZOELINE.

Now I am water-proof.　My fears I can't o'ermaster,
I feel all over like a mild pitch plaster.
What am I tempted to ?　Yet I can't doubt her,
'Tis my disease that I can't live without her.
I would be cured—this step is dangerous, sure,
And oft is fatal—the cold-water cure.
　　　　　　　[*Looks at a pocket glass.*
I'm glad to see my face, it does not soil.
Pah ! it savours strongly of cod's liver oil.

I need not rub my eyebrows, I suppose.
Now for my chin; now I'll touch up my nose.

Enter JOHANNA.

JOHANNA.

Well, Zoeline, to you I am most grateful,
I'm rid of that strange girl, so cold and hateful;
She went this morning to the Rhine, they say,
And brought her robes and ornaments away.
I know this happy change to you is owing——
What are you doing? Whither are you going?

ZOELINE.

To marry Luralie.   Ha, ha! excuse this laughter;
I thought you'd like to throw the slipper after.
Now don't expostulate—no use in sorrow;
I'm sworn to marry Luralie to-morrow.

JOHANNA *sings.*

Faithless, faithless, I was once your idol:
One short month would have dawned upon our bridal;
    But before that time was over,
    Zoeline, Zoeline, you left me for another.

ZOELINE *sings.*

Ah! poor girl, 'tis most distressing,
    Most sincerely I deplore
That, you're charming still confessing,
    Other charms must I adore.

[JOHANNA *and* ZOELINE *sing together.*

JOHANNA.	ZOELINE.
Zoeline, oh, Zoeline,	Luralie, oh, Luralie,
I love none but thee, Zoeline;	I love none but thee, Luralie;
No other claims one thought of mine.	No other can I hear or see.
I love none but thee, Zoeline.	I love none but thee, Luralie.

JOHANNA *sings.*

Think of the Baron's broken-hearted daughter,
Think of the plunge in the cold and sullen water.
    May it haunt you—may it daunt you,
    Zoeline—Zoeline—traitor and deceiver !

                                [*Exit.*

SCENE II.—*The Rhine.* GOBBET *alone.*

GOBBET.

Now is the winter of my mud-born meanness,
Made glorious summer by these people's greenness ;
And now, instead of diving for my meals,
To fright the timid souls of river eels,
And scarcely venturing to bask on shore,
But on a sunny mud-bank grunt and snore,
I drink good beer from foaming pewter mugs,
And sleep in feather-beds, full of nice things called b—gs !
Now for my dinner,—what a jolly mess,
That never wanted cook or fire to dress :
A springing salmon, which I caught myself ;
I'll eat it like a Christian, too, on delf.

                [*Eats at one side of the stage.*

Enter JOHANNA *and* ELSPETH.

ELSPETH.

What would you be a doing, mistress dear?

JOHANNA.

I come to drown myself and sorrows here.

ELSPETH.

You're in your slippered feet—dear mistress, hold—
Do take my shoes, you'll get your death of cold !

Your foot's almost as small as Cinderella,
And, ma'am, why havn't you got your umbrella?
The rain, like rats and mice, is pouring down :
Oh ! 'tis a very ugly night to drown !

JOHANNA.

What nonsense you are talking ! What care I
For rain and cold when I am going to die ?

ELSPETH.

Such folly, mistress dear, ain't you above ?

JOHANNA.

Sure, didn't Dido kill herself for love ?

ELSPETH.

Dido ! she darned her stocking as she sat,
Before the palace gate she *darn't* do that.

JOHANNA.

Here, take my brooch and earrings—you may sell them.
If friends should come to look for me, you'll tell them
They'll find me on the mud-bank down below :
And then "take me up tenderly," don't you know ?

[*Sings ; air, Donna Sabina Waltz.*

    No more hope flushes me,
      Frantic I go,
    Where old Rhine hushes me
      Moaning low.
    There—there grief preyeth not,
      Wasteth not more,
    And old Rhine stayeth not
      Rushing o'er.

ELSPETH *sings.*

Oh, speak to me mildly,
You're staring so wildly,
Your face is so white, dear !
I'm trembling with fright, dear.
Oh, Fraulein ! dear Fraulein ! 'tis fatal, this sadness !
Oh, Fraulein ! dear Fraulein ! your meaning is madness !

You look so despairing,
So vacantly staring !
I'm all in a tremble ;
A ghost you resemble.
Oh, Fraulein ! dear Fraulein ! your meaning is madness !
Oh, Fraulein ! dear Fraulein ! what mean you to do ?

JOHANNA *sings.*

I stay not to ponder, my grave waits me yonder :
To brood in my sorrows one moment I dare not ;
Till soundly I slumber, each moment I number,
I fly from my anguish, and whither I care not.
No more hope flushes me, &c.

JOHANNA *(to Elspeth).*

I know you won't forget my dying wishes :
Now, cruel Zoeline, I'm food for fishes.
[*She jumps into the Rhine.*

ELSPETH.

And so she's drowned herself, and so I let her ;
I greatly fear I'm aider and abetter.
What noise is that ? it frightened me almost.
Alas ! alas ! it is the Fraulein's ghost !
[*She runs off the stage.*

GOBBET.

Though reptile I, she nearly made me blubber.
Here's for a plunge, to save this poor land lubber.

> [GOBBET *dives in after* JOHANNA.

Enter ZOELINE, *all covered with scales.*

ZOELINE.

Oh, horror ! beating every horror hollow !
May the earth open and my body swallow.
I dreamed that to a mermaid I was married,
And to the Rhine in clammy arms was carried ;
I dreamed the monster struck me with her tail,
And all my skin broke out in slimy scale.
Johanna now would loathe me with disgust,
I'll fling me at her feet—I must—I must.

> [*Exit* ZOELINE. *Enter* JOHANNA *and* ELSPETH.

ELSPETH.

It was some crazy door that was a creaking,

JOHANNA.

For shame—the voice was tuneful that was speaking.
I should not now be sorrowful and weeping,
If on the peaceful *mud-bank* I was sleeping ;
It's not so very terrible to drown,
And I was going—oh, so calmly down,
When something seized on my unhappy corpus,
Some kind Newfoundland, or a gentle porpoise,
And brought me softly paddling to the shore.

ZOELINE (*outside*).

Oh, Johanna !

ELSPETH.

Hush, mistress—there again, the creaking door.

Enter ZOELINE.

JOHANNA.

Oh, Zoeline !

ZOELINE.

That's me.

JOHANNA.

Oh, pardon my surprise !
What means that fishy look about your eyes ?
Has some bad spirit your resemblance stole ?
Or is it transmigration of the soul ?
I knew your voice, and hastened to the place,
But scarcely can I recognise your face.
What have you done, that could have changed you so ?

ZOELINE.

I am a crocodile, for all I know ;
And yet no crocodile's tears are those I'm shedding.

JOHANNA.

This should have been the morning of our wedding.

ZOELINE.

My wedding ! name it not, I almost deem
Some charm was over me, some frightful dream—
Some spell that bound me to the cold deceiver ;
'Tis gone, just like—the night-mare of a fever,
And left my heart as once it was, thine own.
What say I—can a reptile's tears atone ?

JOHANNA.

To wed that reptile is my dearest wish.
Give me your hand—[*drops it*]—how clammy, like a fish.
Pardon me, Zoeline ! this is, indeed, felicity ;
The shock I felt must have been Electricity.

I'm happier than the Queen of England now,—
And who knows but you'll some day cast your slough?

ZOELINE.

Dearest Johanna!

JOHANNA.

Yes, what would you say?

ZOELINE.

You know this should have been my wedding day.
I am so hideous, may be you might falter,
And I'm so altered, you might slum the altar—
My reptile face.

JOHANNA.

Dear Zoeline, no more.
I think it's twice as handsome as before.

ELSPETH.

Then what must it have been?   Oh, how she doats!
I think he'd frighten horses from their oats.

ZOELINE.

This generosity I can't repay :
Oh, let this really be our bridal day.

JOHANNA.

With all my heart; dear Zoeline, content;
But shall we ever get Mamma's consent?

ELSPETH.

Into the balance throw his money bales,
And I'll go bail 'twill amply poise the scales.

JOHANNA.

Come, Zoeline, we'll go together now,
And delicately break it to the Frau.

Zoeline *sings ; air, Immortellen Waltz.*

True, still true, faithful are you ;
When all my summer friends left me
You should have left me too.

JOHANNA *sings.*

Still by your side, though all others should leave you ;
Still when the traitor had snared and undone you ;
Proving my constancy, proud to have won you,
Still is my cheering voice heard by your side.

Duet.

JOHANNA.	ZOELINE.
True, still true,	True, still true,
Faithful to you ;	Faithful are you ;
When all your summer friends leave you,	When all my summer friends left me,
Let them desert me too.	You should have left me too.

[*Exeunt.*

Enter LURALIE *in agitation.*

LURALIE.

I've had a dream—a terrible dream.
I thought I heard my old father call;
And his gruff old voice had a threatening tone,
As it thundered up from his sparry hall ;
Thro' Rhine's blue bosom, cold and deep,
I thought I sunk, like a falling star,
Where the light of the sun could hardly peep,
Till it greenly glimmered in caves of spar,
Where the Rhine's green hair kept waving, waving,
And its silent waters were ever laving.
My ears were confused by a gurgling sound ;

The light was dim as when evening closes,
And the goggle-eyed fishes kept prying around,
And bobbing against me with cold clammy noses.
I longed for the cheery voices of men,
The joyous hunt, and the thoughtless wassail;
I longed for the light of the sun again,
The gay greenwood, and the old grey castle.
But the Rhine's green hair kept waving, waving,
And its silent waters were ever laving.
What did I hear in the dancing waves?
My gay young bridegroom, I heard him greet me.
What did I see in the sparry caves?
My gay young bridegroom, I saw him meet me.
"Luralie, long have I waited," he said.
But I sprang with a shriek from his clammy caresses;—
My stern old father was there instead,
And his temples were bound with the Rhine's green tresses,
And the Rhine's green hair kept waving, waving,
And the silent waters were ever laving.

Enter RHINE KING *and* NYMPHS.

RHINE KING.

This is the period that I did appoint thee.
Come! rush to my bosom!

LURALIE.

Dread vision, aroint thee!

RHINE KING.

My power is upon thee, and thou must return.
Come, haste to the water—I burn! I burn!
The tide-wave is rolling, the stars are propitious,—
The sign of the Scales, and the sign of the Fishes.

RHINE KING *sings.*

Haste away! haste away!
Long have I wandered thro' my lonely halls.
Haste away! haste away!
Hark! 'tis the Rhine King calls!

LURALIE *sings.*

Oh, father! bide one falling tide—
The weary waves to seaward glide.
Alas! I cannot, cannot, leave him—leave my Zoeline!

CHORUS OF NYMPHS.

List to our murmuring chorus!
It thrills through the water o'er us.
Oh, come, sister! dearest Luralie!   Oh, dearest Luralie!
Come! we are worn with weeping;—
Our hearts lonely watch are keeping.
Oh, come, sister! dearest Luralie!   Oh, dearest Luralie!

RHINE KING *sings.*

Haste away! haste away!
Long have I wandered thro' my lonely halls.
Haste away! haste away!
Hark! 'tis the Rhine King calls.

LURALIE *sings.*

Oh, father! bide one falling tide—
The weary waves to seaward glide.
Alas! I cannot, cannot leave him—leave my Zoeline!

CHORUS OF NYMPHS.

Lo, thro' the waters gleaming,
Our long robes and tresses streaming—
Oh, come, sister! dearest Luralie!   Oh, dearest Luralie!

List to thy sisters' calling ;
Our wail on thine ear is falling—
Oh, come, sister ! dearest Luralie ! dearest Luralie !

RHINE KING.

Thy chamber awaits thee—all starry and pure :
Thy lamp shall be made of a great Koh-i-noor.
We have banished all things that are slimy and ragged ;
Thy floor shall be coral, thy throne shall be agate,
Thy crown of the wet water-lily and dry rush,
All clustered with diamonds (the diamonds are Irish) ;
And a robe of ice bugles—its tissue is thinnish ;
'Twas completed in Finland with exquisite *finish.*

NYMPH.

Behind thee, sister, see a sunny scene wake.
The spotted trout are jumping at the green drake ;
Your own pet trout has spent itself in leaping
Above the current when it saw you weeping.

LURALIE.

Alas ! What noise ! What mean these acclamations ?

RHINE KING.

Thy Zoeline is false.

NYMPH.

Sister, have patience.
Don't list to the rejoicings of the vain crowd ;
Come, take a shower-bath in yonder rain cloud.

LURALIE.

Father, I come—dear sisters, do not cry ;
My heart's best life's water is nearly dry.
Lull me to sleep with music below,
I'll slumber for a century or so.

When I awake—for time our grief assuages—
We'll find ourselves about the middle ages.
Father, permit me—you can vigil keep :
You know I'm best behaved when I'm asleep ;
You'll see, by peeping downwards thro' the skylight,
My misty figure in the caves' green twilight,
A dreaming of the billows' distant plashes,
All in my clouds of air and long eyelashes.

[Exeunt.

SCENE III.—*A Room in the Castle. Enter* BARON *and* FRAU, *with an immense bill of items, that drags along the floor.*

FRAU.

Now, sir, that she is gone, that nasty viper,
We've had our fun, pray who's to pay the piper ?
Here is an awful bill from the upholsters.

BARON.

Is there an item touching these two bolsters?

[Points to his legs.

FRAU.

The butcher's bill.

BARON.

No more—the bill's a true one.

FRAU.

The bill for wine.

BARON.

'Tis mighty like blue ruin.

FRAU.

The bill for plate.

BARON.

Includes your ugly mug.

E 2

FRAU.

The bill for ale.

BARON.

Will put me in jug.

FRAU.

The bill for trinkets, gewgaws, lace, and rings.

BARON.

One yet—I'll see no more of Banquo's Kings !

Enter JOHANNA, ZOELINE *in scales, and* ELSPETH.

ZOELINE.

I come, good Frau, my humble suit renewing.

FRAU.

Pray, sir, are you the frog that went a wooing?

JOHANNA.

Dear mother, do not thus your son abash :
Father, it merely is a trifling rash.

ZOELINE.

I got it eating lobsters and red pepper.

BARON.

That's a fine bounce—you seem to be a *leper*.

Enter WIZARD.

WIZARD.

I am a man, born of a former race :
My peers are dead, forget my name and place ;
But kindly sympathy, age can't erase.
Friends, I perceive your sad misfortunes clearly.

Alas, poor youth ! I pity you sincerely.
But that you suffered this disgrace was better,
That from your heart might fall her magic fetter.
'Tis true I can't with pharmaceutic skill
Compound the famous " Anti-Scaly-Pill,"
The fame of which, if Holloway but hears,
He'll set the public papers by the ears.
But I can summon from the vasty deep
An able leech.   Ho ! Gobbet, start from sleep !

GOBBET.

Here ! mighty master,—say what is your will.

WIZARD.

Produce the famous " Anti-Scaly Pill,"
And heal this youth, quick, *fugit atra cura,*
I'll then disclose my camera obscura.

GOBBET.

Bid us all hail,—I am a potent wizard ;
You are my subject, now that you're a lizard.
However, we regard you with good will,
And gift you with the " Anti-Scaly-Pill."

JOHANNA.

The " Anti-Scaly-Pill,"—the name is funny.

ELSPETH.

Comfort yourselves, it is not anti-*money.*

GOBBET (*to Baron and Frau*).
Permit their union,—let your squabbles end.

BARON.

And who are you, my most ingenious friend ?

GOBBET.

I am the potentate of slugs and snails,
And all amphibious creatures telling tales ;
Also of bats, and rats, and toads, and frogs,
The Emperor of half a million bogs.

BARON.

Most potent Majesty, pray turn about.
                    [*Kicks him.   Exit* GOBBET.
Ho, I declare, the dog has cured my gout.

ZOELINE.

And cured my scales.   My fortune is my face.
Johanna, lo !

BARON.

Oh, you have changed *the case.*

FRAU.

Dear son-in-law, I greet you with a kiss.

ZOELINE.

Oh, that will do.

FRAU (*kissing him*).

Take this—and this—and this.

BARON.

Of course, young man, the fortune's to the fore.

ZOELINE.

I give her all I have, I can no more.
And you, too, will be generous, no doubt.
What's Fraulein's dowry, Baron ?

BARON.

Oh, my gout!

Enter WILHELM, *who kneels to* FRAU *in mistake for* ELSPETH.

WILHELM.

Forgive me, beauteous maid!

FRAU.

Baron—preserve us!

WILHELM.

I couldn't hang myself, I got so nervous.
Oh! an old woman! Oh, I never knew her!

BARON.

I say, young man, you're very welcome to her.

WILHELM.

Oh, no! My head goes round, my stomach sickens.

BARON.

Try her—she is the tenderest of chickens.

FRAU.

Baron, avenge me, and this ruffian shoot;
                    [*Takes him by the hair.*
I never saw such a ferocious brute.

WILHELM.

Let go my hair, I'll give you such a digging.

BARON.

I knew the poor young man would get a wigging.

ELSPETH.

Good Frau, forgive the poor dear creature—look you,
For your most humble servant he mistook you.
The blunder's natural, for, to be truthful,
Our figures are alike—we both are youthful.
I've seen so much of true love's sorrows lately,

[To WILHELM.

That I quite pity you, and like you greatly.
In fact, unless my mistress is averse,
I'll take you, sir, for better or for worse.

BARON.

Well done, old boys and girls—no more caressing,
You all shall have my patriarchal blessing.

[Takes ZOELINE *aside.*

Now, my gay bridegroom, take this counsel trusty :
Poison your wife when she gets old and crusty.

ELSPETH.

Poor heart ! when an old husband's gout and growls have broke it.

FRAU.

Ha ! Baron,—put that in your pipe and smoke it.

·WIZARD.

You now shall see secure your late tormentor
Asleep for ages in the Rhine's green centre.
There shall she lie till centuries revolve.
Ye mists that dim the mortal eye, dissolve !

Tableau of LURALIE *asleep, the* RHINE KING *and* NYMPHS *standing round her.*

RHINE KING *sings.*

I am frantic—grief gigantic
Harroweth this mighty heaving breast with care.

Pangs tremendous of anguish rend us.
Lo ! how we tear our hoary hair !

CHORUS OF NYMPHS.

Ah ! she sleeps at last.   From our brows we cast
Wreath and flower above her—proving how we love her.
Let us float around, till the spell of sound
Falls on her heart like balm.

RHINE KING *sings.*

Hush this groaning, she is moaning.
Would you scare her slumbers with a funeral strain ?
With glad measure, lull my treasure :
Come, soothe with joyful dreams her pain.

CHORUS OF NYMPHS.

Ah ! howe'er we will, comes a wailing thrill,
      Mingling with her slumbers
      Sad despairing numbers.
Yet we bid thee sleep.   Be thy slumbers deep—
      Sleep till thy heart be calm.

BARON *and* FRAU *sing.*

How romantic—cut an antic.
We behold our hateful foe in limbo there !
Thanks tremendous ! Still defend us
From sprites of water and of air.

CHORUS OF ALL ON THE STAGE.

Chant a bridal song, as we march along ;
      Maidens trip with slim toe,
      Luralie's in limbo !
Thank our hoary friend, with a courteous bend ;
      Thanks, potent, hoary sage.

General Chorus.

RHINE KING *sings.*

I am frantic—grief gigantic
Harroweth this mighty heaving breast with care.
Pangs tremendous of anguish rend us.
Lo! how we tear our hoary hair!

BARON *and* **FRAU** *sing.*

How romantic—cut an antic.
Behold our hateful foe in limbo there!
Thanks tremendous!   Still defend us
From sprites of water and of air.

CHORUS OF NYMPHS.

He is frantic—grief gigantic
Harroweth his mighty heaving breast within.
Pangs tremendous of anguish rend us—
See how he tears his hoary hair!

ELSPETH *comes forward.*

I come to ask your votes for us,
    Most kind and patient friends.
You've had enough of us, perhaps
    You're glad the business ends.
And if you've had a crow to pick,
    No doubt there has been *caws ;*
But drown the sounds of censure
    In your generous applause.

       [Curtain falls.

END OF " LURALIE."

PRINCE CRŒSUS IN SEARCH

OF A WIFE.

BY

THE HON^BLE. MRS. GREENE,

Author of " Cushions and Corners," " The Schoolboy Baronet,"
" Filling up the Chinks," &c. &c.

DRAMATIS PERSONÆ.

KING DE LEAR.
QUEEN LACKADAISICAL (*his wife*).
PRINCESS KATHARINE (*their eldest daughter*).
PRINCESS DELIA (*their youngest daughter*).

MINNA (*waiting-maid to Katharine*).
STYCORAX (*a witch*).
QUEEN'S COUNSELLOR.
PETER SIMPLE (*son to Stycorax*).
PRINCE CRŒSUS.
TWO PAGES.

DRESS.

KING DE LEAR.—Scarlet cloak, bordered with ermine; flowered satin waist-coat; black velvet knee-breeches; scarlet shoes; crown; sword; false beard; white wig; hooked nose.

QUEEN LACKADAISICAL.—Yellow satin dress and train, with demons in black velvet sewn on all round; yellow head-dress and tiara; black lace veil; pocket-handkerchief; eyes red and swollen from crying.

PRINCESS KATHARINE.—White tarletan skirt, flounced, and trimmed with gold braid; crimson tarletan pannier and low body trimmed with broad gold braid; large chignon; necklace; earrings, &c.; white boots.

PRINCESS DELIA.—White tarletan low body and skirt, trimmed with silver braid; blue gauze scarf; silver tiara, and white veil; hair hanging down; white boots.

MINNA.—Dolly Varden pannier over short quilted green petticoat; Dolly Varden cap; green shoes; white stockings; mirror suspended to her waist.

WITCH STYCORAX.—Black silk quilted petticoat, with demons in coloured tinsel paper trimming it; black velvet pannier; hump; crimson cloak, with gold and silver emblems and devices sewn on; high-heeled shoes; high shining hat, trimmed with gold and silver spangles; false nose and chin; broomstick.

QUEEN'S COUNSELLOR.—Black Court suit, with steel buckles; false bald wig; lace ruffles; black silk stockings, and shoes; enormous eyeglass.

PETER SIMPLE.—Blue countryman's blouse; brown knee-breeches; false wig of red hair; gaiters; clogs; false turned-up nose; red cotton handkerchief; stick.

PAGE (*to King De Lear*).—Blue tunic and knee-breeches, slashed with white, trimmed with gold and red braid; cap.

PAGE (*to Prince Crœsus*).—Black tunic and knee-breeches, slashed with yellow, trimmed with gold and red braid.

PRINCE CRŒSUS.—Green doublet and tights, white slashings, trimmed with gold and red braid; scarlet cloak (short), trimmed with ermine or swansdown; scarlet cap to match; white ostrich feather; white silk stockings, with bows of green and red ribbon at the knees; sword; green shoes and diamond buckles.

PRINCE CRŒSUS IN SEARCH OF A WIFE.

ACT I.

SCENE, *King's Palace.* *Enter* KING DE LEAR.

KING.

Yes, yes, 'tis true what ancient Shakespeare said—
Uneasy rests the crown that wears a head.
How many of our subjects at their ease
May wear whatever hat or coat they please !
The Clerics, wide-awake or Tyrolese,
The braided smoking-cap or chimney-pot,
The swallow-tail, frock coat, or paletot.
Of ermined robes our soul is sick and tired,
Yet by unalterable rule it is required.
Our legs in scarlet hose we must encase,
And velvet folds our body shall embrace ;
Wear on our heads a fretting crown of gold,
And in our hands a heavy sceptre hold.
I'll not endure this kingly thraldom more—
I'll dash my sceptre on the palace floor ;
  [Dashes his sceptre on the ground.
My robes of state unto the winds I'll fling,
And cease for evermore to be a king.
  [Throws off his cloak. QUEEN'S *shrieks heard within.*

That melancholy mew, what does it mean ?
Methinks I know the cat : it is the Queen ;
My wretched wife, who makes it her delight
To cry all day, and sob the livelong night.

Enter the PAGE, *and* QUEEN, *and* QUEEN'S COUNSELLOR.

QUEEN.

Alas ! Alack ! Ah me ! ah, well a day:
Was ever seen so bleak, so black a day ?
A racking headache doth my bosom wring ;
Life has no joys for me, nor you, my King.

KING.

Tears, idle tears, I know not what they mean ;
Give me some reason for thy grief, my Queen.

QUEEN.

Tears from the depths of a divine despair :
I gave my satin dress a horrid tear.

                              [Points to her dress.

In haste to tell the news ere 'twas too late—
A horseman armed is standing at the gate,
'Demanding instant audience.

KING.

                       Let him wait
Till we resume these hateful robes of state.

     *[*COUNSELLOR *assists the* KING *to replace his cloak inside out.*
Now let him enter, whosoe'er he be.
[To Queen.]   And look a little bright, my Niobe.

                             [Sound of a bugle.

QUEEN.

Did you hear that ? Hark ! hush—a bugle blast.
De Lear, oh ! hast thou heard ?

KING.

                     I hast, I hast.
Good Counsellor, in this our hour of need,
Do thou advise, and we will give all heed.

Shall we admit this messenger, or not ;
Or shall we tumble him upon the spot ?

QUEEN'S COUNSELLOR.

Most royal King, since you appeal to me,
I cannot for my life the justice see
To tumble one who's on a message sent,
Unless indeed he came to seek for rent ;
Nor would I needless enter on a fight,
Save to support the cause of tenant-right.
Send for the youth, let him his errand tell,
And if it please you, royal sire, why, well ;
If not, let him upon the gallows swing,
Who bears a traitor's message to our King.

QUEEN.

Full well I know a traitor's face he bears.

KING.

How so, my Queen ?

QUEEN.

A traitor's hat he wears ;
Blue is his coat, and orange is his vest.

QUEEN'S COUNSELLOR.

Must all be trait'rous men who thus are dressed ?

QUEEN.

Traitors in every garb bedeck themselves :
Our very hearts are traitors to ourselves.

QUEEN'S COUNSELLOR (aside).

Yes, my good Queen, your words are terse and true ;
Her trait'rous heart turns everything to blue.

QUEEN.

Ah, well I know you make a mock at me.
Like a dim ghost I stand on life's dark sea—
Nothing can give me joy, nothing can make me sad.

KING.

Woman, give o'er, give o'er, you'll drive me mad.
Come hither, Page, no longer I'll delay ;
Orange or green, bid him to walk this way.
[*To Counsellor.*]   Stand you just here, and whisper what to speak.

QUEEN.

I'll stand on this side, for I'm very weak.

> [KING *leans on one arm of* QUEEN'S COUNSELLOR,
> QUEEN *on the other.*

Song—QUEEN'S COUNSELLOR—*Air, "Tommy Dodd."*

> I lead a very tiresome life,
> Like most Queen's Counsellors ;
> I can't get home to see my wife,
> Nor rest in my arm-chair.
> The moment that I turn my back,
> I'm sure to hear the cry—
> " Oh, where's he gone—oh bring him back—
> The great Queen's Counsellor."
> Sometimes it is the weeping Queen—
>   [*In a sobbing voice*] " Counsellor, Counsellor."
> Sometimes it is his Majesty—
>   [*Imperiously*] " Counsellor, Counsellor."
> Sometimes it is the vixen Kate—
>   [*In a sharp, cross voice*] " Counsellor, Counsellor."
> From morn till night 'tis all the same,
> The cry of " Counsellor."

> *Re-enter the* PAGE, *who kneels with a roll in his hand.*

PAGE.

> Most royal sire, ere I could reach the gate
> The porter told me I had come too late ;
> The Knight he gave but two resounding knocks,
> And dropped this roll into the letter-box.

KING (*takes the roll*).

What's this upon the cover?   Let me see :
My name in full, and then " R. S.V.P."
" R. S.V.P.," what can these letters mean ?
" R.S." for Royal Sire, that's easy seen.
But " V." and " P."—it puzzles me a bit.
My learned friend, can you make sense of it ?

QUEEN.

Give it to me : it's meaning well I know.
Rage, Sorrow, Vengeance, Pain—four words of woe.
Open it not, my liege : be warned by me ;
A most felonious plot in it I see.
This roll, no doubt, contains some liquid fire :
Cut but the string, at once we all expire.

QUEEN'S COUNSELLOR.

Madam, your thoughts anticipate the worst.
There is no danger that this roll will burst.
I know full well, by royal tape and string,
It doth contain a message from a King ;
And by the dainty seal and perfumed cover,
I smell a rat—by rat I mean a lover.
These cyphers which the Queen has eyed askance
Come, like all other fashions, straight from France.
Répondez, s'il vous plaît, an answer claims.

KING.

Répondez, s'il vous plaît, are those his names ?

QUEEN'S COUNSELLOR.

I'll ope this roll—his name you'll find inside.

KING (*aside*).

Which pretty daughter will he choose for bride ?

F

QUEEN'S COUNSELLOR (*puts on his spectacles, opens the roll, and reads aloud.*)

" From the most mighty Prince, Imperial Crœsus,
Knight of the Red Cross Band and Golden Fleeces,
To the great King De Lear.   Most royal sire,
Knight of the Whistle and of Vulcan's fire,
Cometh with this our royal love and greeting,
Craving for us and suite a speedy meeting.
The fame of beauty, grace, and temper sweet
Bringeth a suitor to your daughter's feet.
Prince Crœsus, wearied of a single life,
Hath sought at many a court a fitting wife;
A wife with temper sweet and modest air.
[*To the Company*]. Well do we know such qualities are rare.
But many a tongue hath borne us the report
That such a Princess lives within your court;
Her name we know not, though her fame we've heard."

KING.

Delia must be the one; our pretty bird,
Our ingot of pure gold, for Crœsus' mint.
That he may choose aright, I'll give the hint.

QUEEN'S COUNSELLOR.

I wish he'd keep his hints until I've done;
I know not where I stopped, nor where begun.

KING.

Here is the spot, I know the very place.

QUEEN'S COUNSELLOR.

I beg your pardon, and I thank your grace.
[*Resumes.*] "Prince Crœsus by your leave will seek your land,
And crave with humble hope your daughter's hand.
Should the fair Princess (as is only right)
Desire to know our age, our mien, our height,

Our royal father claims this right from me,
As not befitting well our modesty.
I know not what is writ upon the page,
Save that therein he states our rank and age."

KING.

I like the style, and writing too, forsooth—
I think he seems a very worthy youth.
Send for our daughters ere this page we scan ;
The proper study of their sex is man.
For 'twixt them both we shortly must decide
Which of the two we'll give him for his bride.
[*To Page.*] Come hither, Page, and hearken to my speech.
Find out the ladies, and say thus to each :
" Your royal father waits for you below,
And hopes you will most prompt obedience show."
Pause not a moment, e'eu to draw your breath,
Or we will order you to instant death.

QUEEN.

Alas ! Alack ! did not I tell you so ?
Rage, Sorrow, Vengeance, Pain—four words of woe.
Our daughters fair, how can they now agree
Which of the twain Prince Crœsus' bride shall be ?
I am no " Croaker," but, if I read right,
Between the girls there'll be an awful fight :
Kath'rine will storm, and Delia she will weep,
And I, their mother, all the blame shall reap.

KING.

Have patience, Queen : your dark forebodings cease.
I've hit already on a plan for peace.
Something like it I have in Shakespeare read,
And Shakespeare had a most sagacious head.
Full long I've wished my kingdom to resign,
And place these robes on stouter limbs than mine.

My hand is wearied of the guiding helm,
Fain would I now resign both crown and realm.

QUEEN.

What's that he says ?   What can the monster mean ?
Am I to cease as well to be a Queen ?

KING.

Madam, you surely cannot care to reign,
When nothing gives you joy, and nothing pain.

QUEEN.

Again it pleases you to mock at me ;
My tears are nought to you, I plainly see.   [*Weeps.*]

KING.

Before you weep, allow me just one word—
Do not condemn my plan before 'tis heard.
To my two daughters I will put this test :
Which of you girls loves your old father best ?
To their prompt answer we will close attend,
And let their future lot on it depend.
Whichever loves me best shall be the bride,
And have my crown and lands and all beside.

[*Enter the* PRINCESS DELIA, *who comes forward
and, kneeling, kisses her father's hand.*]

Well, pretty daughter, what has brought thee here ?
[*Aside.*]   That *she* will be the one I do not fear.

DELIA.

I came because you called me—that was why ;
And Kath'rine too is coming by and by.

KING.

Ah, by and by.   I do not like those words ;
A parent's wishes should not be deferred.
Why did she wait, nor come at once with thee ?

DELIA.

I told her at the time you'd angry be.
She said that she'd be down quite time enough,
When she had rolled her hair into a puff.

KING.

Bid her at once come down—I cannot wait
While she is dressing up her silly pate.
Go back, my dear, and hasten her descent;
Tell her on prompt obedience I'm intent.

DELIA.

I'll give the message as you bid me do,
Though much I fear my errand I shall rue.

Exit DELIA.

QUEEN'S COUNSELLOR.

Kate's father at a distance scolds apace ;
Wait till they meet each other face to face.

Re-enter DELIA, *weeping.*

DELIA.

She's coming, father, if you'll please to wait.

KING.

Coming ! so's Christmas, tho' tis often late.
But why these tears I see you try to stifle ?

DELIA.

'Twas nothing, father, nothing but a trifle.

Enter KATHARINE, *with a sweeping train.*

KING.

Oh, Katharine !

QUEEN.

Ah, Katharine !

QUEEN'S COUNSELLOR.

Fie, Mistress Kate !

KATHARINE.

How many Katharines more ?   My name I hate.
Was it to "oh," and "ah," and "fie," and frown,
You sent for me in such a hurry down ?
[*To Queen's Counsellor.*]   What have I done to cause your
      sapient sneer ?
The reason of my summons let me hear.

[*Stamps on the ground.*

KING (*hesitatingly*).

My dear, it was the Queen who sent for you.
We thought—at least she thought—it would not do.

KATHARINE.

What would not do ?

KING.

This letter from the Prince.

[KATHARINE *starts.*

QUEEN'S COUNSELLOR.

Ah, saw you that ?   Mark how it made her wince.

KATHARINE.

A Prince ! What Prince ?   Of this I'd like to hear.

KING.

Exactly so : I thought you would, my dear.
A suitor fine, who's coming from the west,
To choose whichever daughter loves—*me*—best.

DELIA *and* KATHARINE.

oves *you* the best !   What can our father mean ?
Explain this riddle.

KING.

You must ask the Queen.

QUEEN.

How very kind of you, my dearest life :
You never tell your riddles to your wife.

QUEEN'S COUNSELLOR (*aside*).

I'm getting rather shy about this test ;
I'm sure curst Kate will say she loves him best.

KING.

Well, girls, no longer will I hide the news :
A bride Prince Crœsus cometh here to choose.

DELIA *and* KATHARINE.

Prince Crœsus comes to choose from one of us ?

KING.

Yes—yes, my dears ; but stop, don't make a fuss.
To damp your spirits I'd be very loth :
Remember this—he cannot marry both ;
So, to save time, I've thought upon a way
That he can make a choice without delay.
But first, before I open up my plan,
You girls must hear what's writ about this man.
Proceed, good friend, and let the ladies know
What kind of fellow seeks to be their beau !

QUEEN'S COUNSELLOR.

With pleasure, Sire. Now listen, ladies fair,
How a good father paints his hopeful heir.

[*Reads from the roll.*

"Our son hath begged that we will herein state
All that doth to his princely mien relate ;
Nothing exaggerate, nor aught set down,
To give a heightened value to his crown.
In this we do agree, for 'twould be silly
To gild refined gold or paint the lily.
Six feet he stands within his royal hose,
Stalwart of make, and yet of graceful pose ;
With Roman nose, and eyes of heavenly hue,
So deeply, darkly, desperately blue ;

With hyacinthine locks and shaven face,
Save where a neat moustache his lip doth grace.
His voice is sweet as any sucking dove."

DELIA.

I feel myself already quite in love.

QUEEN'S COUNSELLOR (*reads*).

'" His manner ever courteous, frank, and bland."

KATHARINE.

I really think he's worthy of my hand.

QUEEN'S COUNSELLOR (*reads*).

" The subject of his truth we need not broach:
A royal Knight, *sans peur et sans reproche*."

[*Closes roll.*

A very good song, and very well sung,
With plenty of butter to the tip of his tongue.
No fear but he'll get a welcome hearty,
This nice young man for a small tea party.

KATHARINE.

Father, *I'm* eldest, and *I* claim the right
To have the first refusal of this Knight :
I do not see why *she* need have a voice.

QUEEN'S COUNSELLOR.

He pays his money, and he takes his choice.
Fair play's a jewel, pretty Mistress Kate.

KATHARINE.

Who spoke to you, you meddling addlepate ?

KING.

The girl is right, the task devolves on me.

QUEEN.

I'm a mere cypher, as you all may see.

DELIA.

Dear mother, 'tis not so ; you must not grieve.
I would not care to wed without your leave.

KING.

Without *my* leave, 'twere better you should say.
My scheme I'll now set forth without delay ;
Nor will I brook a word against this plan,
For *you*, or *she*, or any other man.
Now listen, girls, until I put the test,
Which of you two loves your old father best :
And she who loves me best shall be the bride,
And have my crown and lands and all beside.
Who loves me least must lead a single life,
Nor ever own the tender name of wife.
Katharine, my first-born, hither to my side :
What are thy claims to be the Prince's bride ?

KATHARINE.

And canst thou doubt my love, oh, royal sire ?
Doubt that the moon doth shine, or sun hath fire,
But never doubt my love.　How can I speak,
Where words are foolish and all language weak ?
I love you as the thirsty earth loves rain :
I love you with a love akin to pain :
I love you with a love as deep as death,
A love as lasting as my latest breath.
Is this enough ?

KING.

Nay, nay—not quite, not quite :
You must not share this love with Prince or Knight.
It may sound selfish, but 'tis Shakespeare's plan,
You must not share this love with mortal man.

KATHARINE (*aside*).

The poor old man, how silly he has grown,
To think I may not call my heart my own ;
But though he's silly, he is firm as well ;
I fear I must a little white lie tell,
And say I love him best, though all the while
To win the Prince I'll keep my sweetest smile.
[*To King.*]   Sire, if my heart you still desire to weigh,
Bring in the scales of love without delay ;
Throw in the balance all the weights of " Troy,"
" Apothecaries," " grains," " Avoir du pois ;"
Cast in the mighty Alps to fill the scale,
The Megalosaurus, and the snorting whale ;
Cast in the world itself, with all its weight—
Down comes the scale that holds my love so great.
One ounce of love you'll to my lover spare,
While you shall always have the lion's share.
Is this enough?

KING.

It is enough, and yet it might be more.
Wait till of Delia's heart I probe the core.
Come, pretty chicken, to your parent's call ;
Measure thy love ; thou still may'st have it all.

DELIA.

What words are left with which my love to tell?
And yet methinks thou ought'st to know it well ;
Since as a babe I stood beside thy knee,
Have I not always shown my love to thee?
[*To Queen.*]   And you, who ran to help me when I fell,
And would some piteous story tell,
And kiss the place to make it well,
And tears so plentifully shed,
Upon my little woolly head.   My mother!

QUEEN.

You were indeed a very fractious child,
Your first tooth's tantrums nearly drove me wild.
How oft I've wished that ne'er a child I had,
From first to last it was so very bad.   [*Weeps.*]

KING.

Hence, loathèd melancholy.   Delia, speak,
And never mind your mother's doleful squeak.

DELIA.

What now can I, poor wretched Delia, say ?

KING.

Speak, my good daughter: wherefore this delay ?
I know you love me, but the point is rather
Which will you love the best—husband or father?

DELIA.

I'll tell the truth, whatever it may cost :
Whoe'er I wed, him I must love the most.

KING.

You'll love him best !   Say not that word again.

DELIA.

I must, dear father, though it gives you pain :
Not that I love thee less, but husband more.

KING.

Put her at once outside the palace door.
Better she ne'er were born than vex me so.
My daughter—oh, my daughter, what a blow !
And she is mine, so young and so untender.

DELIA.

So young, my lord, and true.

KING.
                              Away I'll send her.
Her beauty I will mar, her prospects blight :
This instant she shall leave my aching sight.
Now must I vent my wrath or burst with rage.
Stycorax shall do the deed.   Begone, thou Page !
Pause not a moment.   Hither bring the witch ;
To change this graceless girl my fingers itch.

QUEEN.
I knew it would be thus ; I told you so.
Rage, Sorrow, Vengeance, Pain—four words of woe !

KATHARINE.
The silly girl, to draw such anger down :
I, by my tact, have gained both Prince and Crown.

DELIA (*kneels*).
Father, forgive, I do not care to wed :
I will give you Prince Crœsus' love instead.
Let Katharine share with him his royal throne
And I will live for thee, and thee alone !
Here at thy feet I kneel, thy hand I kiss.

KING.
It will not do, base girl ; the test was this :
Love you Prince Crœsus well, your father more.
Come, will you do it ?

DELIA.
                    Never, no never more !
                              [*Thunder, gong, red fire.*
        Enter STYCORAX.
STYCORAX.
Wherefore this hasty summons, King De Lear ?
The dragons wait outside who bore me here.
What is my task ? on whom must fall my blight ?
Hasten, that I may do the deed ere night.

KING.

Here is the maid, here is the faithless child,
Who by her acts has driven her father wild.
All trace of *beauty* from her features tear ;
Instead of diamonds, let her sackcloth wear ;
Within your dismal cave her days shall end ;
No one shall choose her for a wife or friend.
The love she grudged to me, herself may keep,
And, like her mother, she may weep and weep.

QUEEN'S COUNSELLOR.

Sire, pause a moment, ere the deed you rue,
Nor for a crotchet lose a daughter true.
Hearken to me !

KING.

     No, sir, I will not hearken :
My palace doors she never more shall darken.
Take her at once, let her no more delay,
And drag her from this palace far away.

              [WITCH *seizes on* DELIA.

DELIA (*shrieks*).

Father ! oh, father ! mother ! sister dear !

KING.

Don't spare her for her cries.

STYCORAX.

         Oh, never fear.

END OF ACT I.

ACT II.—*A Forest Scene.*

Enter QUEEN'S COUNSELLOR *in great consternation.*

QUEEN'S COUNSELLOR.

What! our sweet Princess! Shame, alas, the pity!
The sweetest chiming bell of all the city.
She whose bright beauty blinded all our sight,
Changed—oh, my garter! to a perfect fright.
And all—and all to—I can scarcely speak—
To gratify a foolish father's freak.
Old doting Tyrant—King I will not call you,
Or else the King of Donkeys I'll instal you.
Oh, my young Princess! Go, thou Prince of snobs,
Weep for thy lost one with thy Queen of sobs!
Even Stycorax, the wretch, was heard to sigh
As her own mischief met her evil eye.
When to a toadstool she had changed the rose,
'Tis said old Stycorax wept and blew her nose.
To think what she is now—what she has been—
Was ever such a transformation seen?
Her eyes, sweet eyes, once all serene like cloisters,
Now goggle horribly like open oysters;
Her mouth, sweet mouth, now hideous grins reveal
Its priceless pearls, her teeth, like orange peel;
Her nose, sweet nose, is now like a potato;
Her face, sweet face, is round like any plate, oh!
Now then, what's to be done—what now remains?
Even I am posed, who carry all the brains.
First of old Stycorax, what is she about?
Ha, ha! she'll wed her to her red-haired lout.
Think of our rose unto a carrot tied;
Think of sweet Delia ugly Peter's bride;

Think of Prince Crœsus, too, with vixen Kate.
Were two such fortunes ever marred by fate !
But hark ! I hear the sound of coming legs—
Prince Crœsus' self, as sure as eggs is eggs.
Here in the shade his coming I will wait,
And see if I can spoke the wheels of fate.

Enter PRINCE CRŒSUS *and little* PAGE. PRINCE CRŒSUS *walks to the*
front of the stage, turns about, and then comes back.

PRINCE CRŒSUS.

To wed !   To take a second self for ever !
I feel just like a bather by the river,
Who shivers, dips his toe, and peers beneath.
The hour is up, and I must take the leap.
Come hither, come hither, my little foot-page ;
You're a cute little fellow, I vow, for your age.
Go down through this wood and bring me the news,
If those buildings we see are King De Lear's mews.

[Exit PAGE.

Again to ponder on my future life :
It is a ticklish thing to choose a wife—
A wife whose heart hangs not on sordid pelf,
But gives true love, aye, for one's very self.
For beauty or rank I care not a pin,
Whether she be fat, or whether she be thin,
Whether she be short, or whether she be tall ;
Let her be good and true—that's all in all.
Yet haply in yon palace walls I'll find
Youth, beauty, rank, and goodness all combined,
If lying rumour speak for once the truth.

QUEEN'S COUNSELLOR (*from the side*).

A very lying cur he is, forsooth !

PRINCE CRŒSUS.

Whence came that voice to break the enchanted spell ?

QUEEN'S COUNSELLOR (*advancing*).

Good morning, sir ! I hope I see you well.

PRINCE CRŒSUS.

Turn, gentle hermit of the dale.
[*Aside.*] A word of counsel sage might now avail.
[*Aloud.*] Good friend, I prithee lend thine ears to me,
And guide my shallop o'er this troublous sea.
Here in a foreign land alone I roam.

QUEEN'S COUNSELLOR.

Seek not in yonder hall to find a home.

PRINCE CRŒSUS.

How so ?

QUEEN'S COUNSELLOR.

Nothing.   Oh, nothing ! prithee let me pass.

PRINCE CRŒSUS.

Now by thy cockle hat thou art an ass.

QUEEN'S COUNSELLOR.

Now by thy foppish air thou art a prince,
And therefore from advice art sure to wince.
To guide thy shallop thou didst ask my hand ;
But when I touched the helm at thy command,
Straightway thy temper rose—but what care I,
Whether in quicksands near you choose to die ?
Those who push on where danger signals flame,
Have, when they come to grief, themselves to blame.

PRINCE CRŒSUS.

Whoe'er he be, I'd better change my tune.
The hours are flying fast—'tis nearly noon ;
And they'll expect me at the palace gate.
A lady's in the case—I cannot wait.

Most noble, grave, and reverend Signor, list :
Give me your hand, and with your brain assist.
To yonder halls my erring steps are bent.

QUEEN'S COUNSELLOR.

To find a wife is plainly your intent.

PRINCE CRŒSUS.

What does he mean ? Methinks he's over wise.

QUEEN'S COUNSELLOR.

I read your little secret in your eyes,
So deeply, darkly, desperately blue.
Your errand, noble sir, is there to woo.

PRINCE CRŒSUS.

Just so, and I will ask for some advice.

QUEEN'S COUNSELLOR.

Make not a throw before you weigh the dice.
In yonder halls all is not gold that glitters,
And silvered pills are often filled with bitters.

PRINCE CRŒSUS.

His words a tremor send through all my frame.
Who is this bitter pill ? I'll ask her name.
Proceed, for, like the learned pig of old,
I see you can a lengthy tale unfold.

QUEEN'S COUNSELLOR.

A donkey first, forsooth, and now a pig.
For Delia's sake why should I care a fig ?

PRINCE CRŒSUS.

Delia ; is that the girl you seem to hate ?

QUEEN'S COUNSELLOR.

Nay, nay, good sir, I spoke of Mistress Kate ;
Pretty Miss Kate, with all her tricks and wiles,
Who's laid a plot to snare thee with her smiles.

G

PRINCE CRŒSUS.

How can you tell, who know not e'en my name?

QUEEN'S COUNSELLOR.

Doth not the whole world ring with Crœsus' fame
I tell you what, good friend, the trap is set,
And Mistress Kate will catch you in her net.
No greater conquest could the vixen crave
Than to have you, great Crœsus, for her slave.

PRINCE CRŒSUS.

Is this the case, and have I hither strayed
To fall a victim to a shrewish maid?
How can I tell if you are speaking truth?

QUEEN'S COUNSELLOR.

Here is an answer to your doubts, forsooth :
Up through the wood the Princess wends her way ;
Step here aside, and watch her little play.

      [*They retire behind the trees at opposite sides of the stage.*

Enter KATHARINE, *followed by* MINNA *dressed as a waiting-maid,
with a small hand mirror tied to her belt.*

Song—KATHARINE (*to the tune of "Clochette"*).

I am a sad coquette,
    Prince Crœsus is coming to woo.
That he will love me truly
    I have no doubt—have you?

KATHARINE.

This way he ought to come, the lazy loon.

MINNA.

Indeed, dear mistress, he is coming soon.
I heard a bugle in the forest near.

KATHARINE (*boxes her ears*).

Did you hear that? I'll mend your stupid ear.

MINNA.

Indeed it won't ; it's broken it instead.
[*Aside.*] This mistress makes me wish that I were dead.

KATHARINE.

How shall I stand when the great Prince appears ?

MINNA.

How can I tell ? my eyes are full of tears.

KATHARINE.

Shut up, you silly, or I'll dry them soon :
And don't go winking like a young baboon.
Is my hair tossed ? Come, hand me quick the glass.
Oh, but you are a butter-fingered lass.
Just look at this ! I knew 'twas tossed outright ;
The wind has blown it all about in spite.
Well, never mind ; nothing can spoil my grace—
Each man must die of love who sees my face.
What of my pannier ? is it sticking out ?
There now, you silly girl, don't go and pout.

MINNA.

I cannot help : I'm sure I try to please,
And yet you never cease to scold and tease.

KATHARINE.

Well, and what harm, for are not you my slave ?
And yet, with all my pains, you can't behave.

MINNA.

My pains she means.   When will this torment end ?

KATHARINE.

Now, Minna, look at me : have I the Grecian bend ?
[*Walks across the stage.*

G 2

MINNA.

Yes, Mistress Kate ; your walk is light and airy.
[*Aside.*] Her back is humped just like a dromedary.

KATHARINE.

How shall I look when I Prince Crœsus meet ?
Will the rouge stir if with a kiss he greet ?
Will he find out I paint ?

MINNA.

           Oh, mistress, never !
He'll only think you beautiful for ever.

KATHARINE.

Shall I look pensive, like a violet sweet ;
Or shall I bring him trembling to my feet ?

MINNA.

Take my advice, try on no silly art ;
'Tis cruel work to break a noble heart.

KATHARINE.

To break his heart, why, that is just the fun :
I only wish the sport were well begun.

MINNA.

The Lady Delia would not trifle so ;
She has a heart that feels for others' woe.

KATHARINE.

I'll make you feel, whether she feels or not.
Now you shall catch it, trust me, pretty hot.

                        [*Strikes her.*

Take that—and that—and yet another smack ;
I'll beat you till your body's blue and black.
Ah, Mistress Minna, now I think you wince.

MINNA.

Alas ! Alack ! the poor, unhappy Prince !

KATHARINE.

The Prince! I cannot guess what keeps him so.
Back to the palace I will instant go ;
And this I vow, when once this Prince I marry,
Both head and heart I'll break, if thus he tarry.

[*Exeunt* PRINCESS *and* MINNA. *Enter* PRINCE CRŒSUS
and QUEEN'S COUNSELLOR.

PRINCE CRŒSUS.

I have not words, good sir, to speak my thanks,
That you this ambush gave to watch her pranks.
The fun she looks for, she must now forego.
To break my heart!   Well, rather "not for Joe!"
But what of Delia?   Twice I've heard the name,
And I must turn my thoughts to other game.

QUEEN'S COUNSELLOR.

Delia : only a poor girl living in the wood.

PRINCE CRŒSUS.

Poor !   What care I, if only she be good ?

QUEEN'S COUNSELLOR.

But she has got no charms of face to boast ;—
Nothing but virtue.

PRINCE CRŒSUS.

In itself a host.

QUEEN'S COUNSELLOR.

But she is simple as a little child ;
Too easily her heart might be beguiled.
Therefore I pray you, Prince, to let her be
In maiden meditation fancy free.

PRINCE CRŒSUS.

Nay, at this girl I'd like to have a look ;
She seems exactly suited to my book.

Where is her dwelling?   Prithee point the way :
While the sun shines, 'twere better to make hay.

QUEEN'S COUNSELLOR.

No sun doth shine where wretched Delia lives ;
She hath no food or clothes [*Prince starts*], save what old
    Stycorax gives.
Old Stycorax—foul witch, the country's blight—
Hides in her cave this rare pearl from our sight.
If that you'd brave her ire, and seek her cave,
You might, perhaps, the luckless damsel save.

PRINCE CRŒSUS.

And I will save her, if this arm hath power,
And give her all my love and all my dower.

QUEEN'S COUNSELLOR.

Pause just a moment, Prince, while this I say :
Old Stycorax hath a son, now far away,
But coming home across the dark blue sea,
And if you don't look sharp, he'll marry she.
This is no idle threat, for well I know,
Old Stycorax tied this string unto her bow.

PRINCE.

Hark ! who comes here ?

QUEEN'S COUNSELLOR.

           My ancient neck I'll stretch.
'Tis Peter, as I live—the ugly wretch !

PRINCE CRŒSUS.

Could not we stop him, and some plan devise
To throw some dust into his ferret eyes ?

QUEEN'S COUNSELLOR (*meditating*).

I have a plan : leave now the task to me,
And you shall shortly see—what you shall see.

Enter PETER SIMPLE, *singing, with a stick in his hand, and a bundle tied up in a red cotton pocket-handkerchief.*

QUEEN'S COUNSELLOR.

Where are you going to, my pretty man ?

PETER SIMPLE.

To see my mother as fast as I can.

QUEEN'S COUNSELLOR.

And what is your fortune, and what is your luck ?

PETER SIMPLE.

My face is my fortune, you curious old buck.

QUEEN'S COUNSELLOR.

And what is your trade, and what are you doing ?

PETER SIMPLE.

My trade is to fight, and my pastime is wooing,
If more you would know of my craft and my rigging,
I've come home for a wife to take home to my digging.
There's a nice little girl, as I hear, at our house,
Who, my mother writes word, is as meek as a mouse.
I hate all meek women, for the matter of that ;
And what is still worse, she's as poor as a rat.

[*Sings.*

A spaniel, a wife, and a walnut-tree,
The more you beat them, the better they'll be.

QUEEN'S COUNSELLOR.

The very man for Katharine.   Peter, wait :
What would you say to marry Mistress Kate ?

PETER SIMPLE.

Marry, forsooth, I'd ask for nothing better :
I only wish you'd show me how to get her.

QUEEN'S COUNSELLOR.

'Tis easy done, save for your ugly face,
For of this Prince you'll have to take the place.

This Prince to marry Kate has crossed the sea ;
On second thoughts he'd rather let her be.
Up at the palace now they wait for him :
Change clothes with him, old boy, go in and win,
Put on his hat, his coat, his breeches too ;
You're just the cut of man Miss Kate to woo.
The King's a booby, and the Queen's a fool,
And in that court none but Miss Kate to rule ;
A very shrew she is, but I suppose——

PETER SIMPLE.

Oh, if that's all, I'll lead her by the nose.
I'm not afraid of her, but of her dad,
For if he found me out he would be mad.

QUEEN'S COUNSELLOR.

Oh, never fear, I'll manage that for you :
I'll tame the King, if you will tame the shrew.

PETER SIMPLE.

To learn my part I must at once begin.
I know the dodge to break the grey mare in ;
But as I never in a palace stood,
I am afraid I'd be a trifle rude.
A courtier's ways are quite unknown to me ;
I wish he'd make his face a loan to me.
How shall I enter ? Shall I bow and scrape,
And point my toe like yonder jackanape ?
Come, hither, youth ; teach me to mouth and mince ;
Give me some foolish talk to suit a Prince.

PRINCE CRŒSUS.

Your manners, gentle youth, no polish needs ;
Your language, too, my flow of words exceeds :
Your handsome face, and bearing so polite,
Are sure to slay the Princess at first sight.

PETER SIMPLE.

All this I know ; I'm sure that I shall please,
But want some hints to put me at my ease.
Once I am set afloat, I'll pull along :
Teach me to cut a joke, or sing a song ;
When I'm to kneel, or when I am to rise,
When to speak truth, and when to tell some lies.

PRINCE CRŒSUS.

When first you enter, you can kneel down thus.
   [PRINCE *kneels ;* PETER *spreads the red pocket-handkerchief*
     on the ground and flops down beside him.
Exactly so, but without so much fuss :
Then lift your hat unto the ladies fair,
That each may see your lovely auburn hair :
Then rise up—so—and lean upon your sword.
     [PETER *leans in a ridiculous way upon his stick.*
You could not do it better, 'pon my word ;
A very Prince you are in every feature.

PETER SIMPLE.

I always was a very lovely creature.
Now put some honey on these lovely lips,
Lest in my talk I make some awkward slips :
Give me some sentence that will please the King—
I don't exactly know the kind of thing

PRINCE CRŒSUS.

" *Comment vous portez-vous ?* " perhaps would please ;
" *Pardonnez-moi* " if that you chance to sneeze.
If that your birth or truth the King should broach,
Say you're a Knight *sans peur et sans reproche.*
If they demand a song, why sing, of course :
Something like this, I think, would suit your voice.
     [*Sings* " *Voici le sabre de mon père.*"

PETER SIMPLE.

That's a very nice song—I suppose it is new ;
I'd like something better, with tooral-lu-lu.
Now tell me, my friend, if this wouldn't do.

[*Sings " The Ratcatcher's Daughter."*

PRINCE CRŒSUS.

That's a very high song, but very low art.

PETER SIMPLE.

Excuse me, good sir, it's by Mr. Mozart.
If one won't answer, t'other then will do.
And now that I am up to a trick or two,
Let's spread our sails and dexterously tack ;
You hoist " Blue Peter," I the " Union Jack."
Here, give your hat, and now, young cove, your cloak ;
We'll change our pantaloons behind this oak.

[*Exeunt.*

QUEEN'S COUNSELLOR *sings ; air, "Walking in the Zoo."*

Now if my plan succeeds, as well it ought to do,
Delia will get the Prince, and all his riches too.
And pretty Mistress Kate will get her portion too,
For Peter Simple he's the man to win and tame a shrew.
          Taming of the shrew,
          Taming of the shrew,
Now, gentlemen, you'll get a hint how Peter tames his shrew.

END OF ACT II.

ACT III.—*Interior of a Cavern.*

WITCH *seated by a spinning-wheel.   She rises and walks round a cauldron of fire.*

WITCH.

Round about the cauldron go,
In the poisoned entrails throw,
Wing of frog and toe of snail,
> [*Throws red fire into the cauldron.*
Fin of cat and leg of whale.
Parrots' teeth and fishes' claws,
Sucking doves and pigeons' paws.
> [*Throws blue fire into the cauldron.*
Double, double, toil and trouble,
Bubble and squeak, and squeak and bubble.
Round I stir the savoury stew,
And my best of victuals brew,
For the darling of my eyes,
He who homeward hither flies ;
Better still I have in store,
Which will please him more and more—
Peter, my sweet son and heir,
He shall wed a Princess fair.
Petery Pan, he is the man
To carry out my nice little plan,
With his lovely nose and his carrotty hair,
He shall marry Miss Delia fair.
No man on earth hath e'er done better
Since Peter Piper picked his peck of pepper.
Just of one little thing I am afraid,—
Have I the little girl too ugly made.
Did I, in sportive mood, her so ungrace,
That all will shudder when they see her face ?

No matter.   By the nature of my spell,
There is a chance that all will still go well.
If one should love her for her very self,
Without a thought of rank or sordid pelf,
Just for her virtues, and her temper kind,
Her gentle nature, and her modest mind;
If that her ugly face no difference make,
Nor in his purpose does the lover shake,
Then is the web I wove asunder torn,
And all her pretty charms to her return.
But Peter must not know her rank or race,
Or that she really hath a pretty face,
Or that some day she may an heiress grow,
For though he's fond of virtue, this I know :
Should he but guess the girl hath any pelf,
He'd love the money better than herself.
I first must leave the girl to work her way,
And just this once give innocence fair play.
Now, by the pricking of my gouty thumbs,
My much-loved Peter surely hither comes.

        | *Timid knocking at the door.*

Nay, what a tap he gives, like any mouse.
Walk in, my Peter, to your mother's house.

  [PRINCE CRŒSUS *enters,* *dressed in* PETER's *clothes.*   WITC
   rushes at him, and folds him in her arms.

Peter! Peter! Peter! oh, my long-lost son

    PRINCE CRŒSUS (*aside*).

This is a trial sore for any one.

      WITCH.

Come, Peter, to your mother's skinny arms.

    PRINCE CRŒSUS (*aside*).

This awful hag my very soul alarms.
Must I this old crone woo to win my wife ?
I could not do it, not to save my life.

WITCH.

Peter, my dearest son, how shy you've grown :
You cannot wish your mother to disown ?
And you, who've been so very long away,
And I, who've watched for you both night and day.
It is not kind of you to treat me so.

PRINCE CRŒSUS.

Madam, I—I really did not know.

WITCH.

Don't call me Madam—it is very rude.

PRINCE CRŒSUS.

I meant it for respect.

WITCH.

That's very good.
I'd rather have one kiss than all this folly.
Come, Peter, try and look a little jolly.

PRINCE CRŒSUS.

I am quite jolly, I assure you, Ma'am.

WITCH.

Ma'am   do you Ma'am me ?

PRINCE CRŒSUS.

Well, ain't you my mammy ?

WITCH.

I am your mammy, you my darling son.
My ! what a beauty, Peter, you have grown !
You've quite a handsome face, and noble air ;
But what's become of all your lovely hair ?

PRINCE CRŒSUS.

My hair ! why, is it not upon my head ?

WITCH.

Oh yes, my Peter, but it once was red.

PRINCE CRŒSUS.

Ah, yes, I now remember; 'twas a wrench :
I sold it to the Empress of the French—
'Twas the high fashion for a time at Court—
And at another shop this wig I bought.
[*Aside.*] When will this odious woman leave the place ?
To tell more lies I have not got the face.

WITCH.

Don't, pretty darling, turn your face aside.
I've found you, Peter, such a charming bride.
If you won't look at me, you'll look at her :
Nor will I long your happiness defer ;
I'll call her straight,—but listen, Peter dear :
A word I now must whisper in your ear.
Don't be particular when you're going to woo,
Don't look for miracles ; few wise men do.
A girl who's good and true, howe'er so plain,
Will seldom give her lover cause for pain.

PRINCE CRŒSUS.

In this I quite agree.   Send me the maid.

WITCH.

Yes, that I will, unless she's been delayed.
I sent her to the market, eggs to buy ;
She may not have come back—I'll go and try.
    [*Goes towards the door, then turns and rushes towards the* PRINCE.
Oh, Peter, one more kiss before we part.

PRINCE CRŒSUS.

Oh, mercy ! one more kiss would break my heart.
                                        [*Exit* WITCH.
Had ever wretched Prince to use such art ?
I do repent me of this acted part.

I cannot to this hag true love evince,,
And yet my coldness makes her poor heart wince.
Shall I this moment snatch, and leave this den ?
Back to the Castle hie, and then—and then—
To be or not to be—aye, there's the rub !
Whether to wed the butterfly or grub.
No rose upon the earth without a thorn ;
And what is beauty when of goodness shorn ?
        [*Door opens ; enter* DELIA *with hat on and veil drawn down.*
A tidier lass I never saw before.

DELIA.

Good evening, sir.

PRINCE CRŒSUS.

                    Pray let me shut the door.
You've been a marketing, as I do guess,
Both by your little hat and dainty dress ?

DELIA.

Yes, for some eggs and butter I was sent.

PRINCE CRŒSUS.

The pretty lass, on household cares intent.
And are you tired with carrying such a load ?
        [DELIA *takes off her hat and veil ;* PRINCE *recoils in horror.*
Did ever eyes behold such face of toad ?
Now in a pretty way my hands are tied ;
I could not, could not take her for my bride.

DELIA.

And are you Peter who was coming home ?

PRINCE CRŒSUS.

Yes, I am Peter, who abroad did roam.

DELIA.

Your mother is so glad to see you back !

PRINCE CRŒSUS.

Each artless word does my poor bosom rack.

DELIA.

And does your mother know that you are *in ?*

PRINCE CRŒSUS.

Yes, she went out to call you to come in.

DELIA *sits down at the spinning-wheel and sings.*
Air, " I built a bridge of fancies."

She sent me to the market,
　To buy some eggs and butter ;
She does not know, poor woman,
　How my sad heart doth flutter.
How many a time I weep,
　For all the joys of home ;
Oh ! could she know the pain,
　She'd ask me not to roam.
How oft I sit and spin,
　While the blinding tears run down,
And think of my old mother,
　And all the friends at home.
Oh, could I only see them
　For one short hour again !
Oh, could I only clasp them,
　To ease my heart of pain !

PRINCE CRŒSUS.

Poor girl ! her voice is soft, gentle, and low,
An excellent thing in woman.   Yet I know
'Twere hard to love her.   Little one—I say—

DELIA.

Sir, did you speak ?

PRINCE CRŒSUS.

　　　　Yes, yes—'tis a fine day.

DELIA.

Yes, it is very fine ; the air is sweet.

PRINCE CRŒSUS.

Did you perchance this morn your lover meet ?

DELIA.

I meet my lover !—that were hard to do,
Since not a man on earth my hand doth woo ;
I have no beauty—neither winning grace.

PRINCE CRŒSUS.

All beauty is not summed up in a face.

DELIA.

Nay, that is true, but I am poor as well ;
I have not got one charm that makes a belle.

PRINCE CRŒSUS.

You have a pleasing voice, and manner sweet ;
A pretty little dress, and figure neat.

DELIA.

Ah ! all my wardrobe is not much to boast.

PRINCE CRŒSUS.

Beauty when unadorned 's adorned the most.

DELIA.

Do not, I pray, sir, make a jest at me :
You're trying just to make the best of me.
I'd rather now you told the honest truth,
And said I was a hideous girl ; forsooth,
I know I am—I see it in the glass.

PRINCE CRŒSUS.

Well, now, you are an honest little lass ;
Come, draw your chair near mine,—we'll have a chat.
Here, wait a moment, till I move my hat.

[*They sit down.*

DELIA (*aside*).

I did not think that Peter 'd be so kind,
Or that a peasant could be so refined.
[*Aloud.*] And did it take you long to cross the sea ?

PRINCE CRŒSUS.

To me it seemed quite an eternity ;
For I was coming home to seek a bride.
                    [DELIA *folds her hands, and sighs.*
[*Aside.*] I almost think the little lassie sighed.
[*Aloud.*] Why turn your head, and wherefore that low sigh ?

DELIA.

My thoughts had wandered to a time gone by.

PRINCE CRŒSUS.

What kind of time, pray ? was it good or bad ?

DELIA.

I only know just this—'twas very sad.

PRINCE CRŒSUS.

How so, sweet maid ?   Confide thy grief to me ;
You'll find how good a confidant I'll be.

DELIA.

Of that I'm sure, I read it in your face ;
All your kind wish, I in your features trace.
But grief like mine were better hidden far ;
Why should my sorrow your first meeting mar?

PRINCE CRŒSUS.

What meeting, then ?   What meeting do you mean ?

DELIA.

Your mother, Peter.

PRINCE CRŒSUS.

            My mother I have seen.
In her fond arms thrice has she held me close,
Nor crave I repetition of the dose.

DELIA.

Oh that my mother's arms might me enfold !
Oh that my father's eyes might me behold !
Oh that this mask might drop which hides my face,
That I might feel again his fond embrace.
Oh that Prince Crœsus ne'er had crossed the sea !
I in my parents' home might happy be.

PRINCE CRŒSUS.

What did she say ?   My name I surely heard.
Did you Prince Crœsus name, my pretty bird ?

DELIA.

And if I did, 'twere foolish of me now :
I will not speak his name again, I vow ;
'Tis full of every thought that drives me mad.

PRINCE CRŒSUS.

Why, how so, girl ? is he so very bad ?

DELIA.

Nay, he is goodness' self, from what I hear ;
And for *his* happiness I also fear.

PRINCE CRŒSUS.

How so ?   I've heard he weds the Princess Kate.
What cause have you thus to lament his fate ?
Is she not pretty, rich, and passing fair ?
Hath she not virtue great and temper rare ?
Do you the Princess envy for her choice ?

DELIA.

Sir, in this matter how can I have a voice ?
I envy none, nor would I Crœsus own :
I only sigh for what was once my home ;

H 2

For parents dear, for loving, happy days,
For childhood's freedom, and for childhood's plays ;
Here in this den a lonely life I lead,
Where I might live and die, and no one heed.

PRINCE CRŒSUS.

And is this odious hag to you unkind ?

DELIA.

She is your mother, Peter.

PRINCE CRŒSUS.

              Never mind.
Tell me the truth : are you unhappy here ?

DELIA.

Nay, for my happiness you need not fear.
If that she scolds me much, abroad I roam :
She will be better now that you are home.
She is not bad at heart, I do believe,
But wept for you from morn till dewy eve.

PRINCE CRŒSUS.

You are too good, too full of pity sweet.
Here let me kneel a suppliant at your feet.

DELIA.

Nay, sir, I beg you'll rise from off the floor.

PRINCE CRŒSUS.

I tell you, pretty maid, I you adore.

DELIA.

Pretty ! you're mocking—now you are unkind.

PRINCE CRŒSUS.

Have you not heard, sweet maid, that love is blind ?
Your face, I own, is just a little plain,
But a love given to beauty I disdain.

Your goodness is a beauty in itself,
More to be coveted than rank or wealth.
Will you now take a poor but honest heart,
And give this promise, ne'er from me to part ?

DELIA.

He offers me his hand—what can I say?
I can't say " Yes," and yet I can't say " Nay."
Since first I raised the latch and oped the door,
I felt I had not seen his like before.

PRINCE CRŒSUS.

I see you love me ; try not to deceive.

DELIA.

I cannot wed without my father's leave.

Enter WITCH, *triumphantly.*

WITCH.

Your father's leave you'll have, my pretty chick.
Peter, you've made a conquest wondrous quick.
I did not think my Peter had such charms,
To lure a pretty Princess to his arms.
Lest his quick wooing he should quick repent,
I'll have a message to the palace sent.

[*Exeunt.*

END OF ACT III.

ACT IV.—*The Palace.*

KING *and* QUEEN.   KATHARINE *seated, in a pout.*   MINNA.   KING *advances to* KATHARINE.

KING.

Now, my sweet Kate, I prithee cease to pout :
Such constant fretting, love, will wear you out.
Try to look cheerful, coax a pretty smile :
The Prince will surely come,—just wait a while.

KATHARINE.

Wait !   I am sick of waiting,—foolish stuff.
I've waited for this Prince quite long enough.

MINNA.

She talks of waiting,—think of *me*, poor jade,
Who always must remain a *waiting* maid.

KATHARINE.

What did you say, you pert, provoking child ?
Such prating in my ear will drive me wild.
Would that I now this laggard Prince might catch ;
His very eyes from out his head I'd scratch.

MINNA.

Oh, the poor Prince, would that I him could warn,
Ere from his head his lovely eyes are torn.

KATHARINE.

You spoke again.

MINNA.

No, no.

KATHARINE.

Yes, yes, you did.

MINNA.

And mayn't I speak?

KATHARINE.

No, not unless you're bid.
Go, from the window cast another glance,—
Whom do you see?

MINNA.

A Knight with sword and lance.
It is the Prince, indeed it is, Miss Kate.

KATHARINE.

I'm sure it's not; he would not come so late.

MINNA.

Ah, 'tis the Prince, I see his trappings gay,
And our Queen's Counsellor is showing him the way.
He has a little page, a sword, and gun,
And such a beauteous nose,—my eyes, what fun!

KATHARINE.

What's that you said, you insolent young minx?
I'll make *your* nose like the Egyptian Sphinx.

QUEEN.

Alas! Alack! did not I tell you so?
Rage, Sorrow, Vengeance, Pain—four words of woe!

KING.

Dry up your tears, you weeping crocodile!
And you, young Kitty, try and coax a smile.

MINNA.

Oh, such a youth I never, never saw.

KATHARINE.

What is he like?

MINNA.

Well, just a little raw.

KATHARINE.

You silly goose, what kind of judge are you?

MINNA.

Judge for yourself whether my words are true.

Enter QUEEN'S COUNSELLOR.

QUEEN'S COUNSELLOR.

My liege, my lady, and my Princess fair,
Prince Crœsus is arrived, and on the stair.
His journey was delayed by adverse fate;
He begs forgiveness that he comes so late,
And prays, great Princess, that you'll gently scan
The physique of this sea-sick, love-lorn man.

QUEEN.

Physic! poor youth, had he applied to me,
I have some lovely globules for the sea.

KATHARINE.

For goodness' sake, Ma, stop this silly prating:
Did you not hear the Prince outside is waiting?
And you, sir, standing there and taking snuff,
Of your old babbling tongue we've had enough.

QUEEN'S COUNSELLOR *bows, and says in a stentorian voice, as* PETER
enters dressed in PRINCE CRŒSUS' *clothes :*

Allow me to announce the great Prince Crœsus,
Knight of the Red Cross Band and Golden Fleeces.

[*All the party bow profoundly.* PETER *remains standing
with his hat on, in a state of bewilderment.*

KATHARINE.

Oh, mercy! such a Prince did eyes e'er see?

MINNA.

He does not boast of much civility.

PETER SIMPLE (*aside*).

What shall I say ? I'm getting in a fright:
My eyes are dazzled with the sudden light.

KING.

Rise, my good friend ! my royal Crœsus, rise ;
You are most welcome to our kingly eyes.

PETER SIMPLE (*aside*).

What shall I say ? my brains I must keep cool.
Hallo ! I recollect.   [*Aloud.*] Come on, you portly fool.

KING.

Odds bobs and daggers !   What's the fellow at ?
[*Aside.*] He neither knows to kneel nor lift his hat.
Still, as to marry him our Kate is set,
We will not quarrel over etiquette.
Great Crœsus ! see, this is my daughter fair ;
Beside her will you please to take a chair ?

PETER SIMPLE.

Which is the lovely girl that I'm to wed ?

QUEEN'S COUNSELLOR.

This is the Princess ; *this* the waiting maid.

PETER SIMPLE.

I see no difference—both to me are best ;
They're both so well got up and grandly dressed.

[KATHARINE *turns away, and tosses her head.*

KATHARINE.

Was ever such a fish brought in to shore ?
[*Aside.*] Save for his golden scales, I'd throw him o'er.
[*Aloud.*] So you're the great Prince Crœsus from abroad !
Much of your style and beauty we have heard.

PETER SIMPLE.

And how do you like me, now you see my face ?

KATHARINE.

I neither see the beauty nor the grace.

KING.

Hush, Kitty, try and keep your temper down ;
You don't look pretty with that angry frown.

KATHARINE.

I cannot help it, father, he's so rude.

KING.

A sea-sick passage may have caused this mood.

KATHARINE.

I'll change his mood if he be left to me.

QUEEN.

The girl is right—alone they ought to be.
When we were young it always was the way,
To let the lovers have their little say.
How oft, when we were young, we've wept together.

KING.

Pray don't remind me of that showery weather.
The day was cold and dark, and very dreary,
When you made love to me, my ancient deary.

PETER SIMPLE.

Now, my good sir, I prithee clear the way :
This little girl and I must have our say.
Your recollections are most fond, O King !
But just at present they are not the thing.

KING.

In all my life I never—no, I never.

QUEEN.

In all my life I never—no, I never.

KING.

Yet, on the whole, perhaps it might be better.
Farewell, my dears! I've got to write a letter.
          [*Exeunt* KING, QUEEN, *and suite;* PETER *looking after them.*

PETER SIMPLE.

Their room is better than their company.
                    [*Throws himself into an arm-chair.*
Now, want of company, welcome trumpery.
Nay, what a toss she gives her pretty head.

KATHARINE.

I have not listened to a word you said.

PETER SIMPLE.

So much the better, love, my words are few;
Should I repeat myself, 'twill sound quite new.

KATHARINE.

So coarse a looking man I never saw.
Minna was right when she pronounced him raw.

PETER SIMPLE.

Come, Kitty, turn your saucy little face.

KATHARINE.

How dare you call me Kitty? Leave the place.

PETER SIMPLE.

Don't take on so—there is no use in life;
You know you are to be my loving wife.

KATHARINE.

I'd like to see myself.

PETER SIMPLE.

            Well, come and try;
You'll find your sweet reflection in my eye.

KATHARINE.

Of all the hateful men I ever met,
You are the worst.

PETER SIMPLE.

                    Well, that's true, my pet.
Of every beauteous form you are the type.
See here, my little girl, come, light my pipe.

> [QUEEN'S COUNSELLOR *and* MINNA *sneeze violently.*
> PETER *leaps up from his arm-chair.*

I say! what's that! Oh, is it you, old boy,
And you, young person, whom I thought so coy?
Have you been listening to our conversation,
Or having, on the sly, your own flirtation?
Whichever is the case, I beg you'll walk,
And leave Miss Kate and me to have our talk.
The course of true love always runs the quicker,
When not obstructed by a daisy picker.

KATHARINE.

I will not have them go.   Stay, Minna, stay.

PETER SIMPLE.

This instant, when I bid you, go away.

MINNA.

Which shall I do? of Mistress I'm afraid.

KATHARINE.

I bid you stay with me—you are my maid.

PETER SIMPLE.

When I say "Go," she must at once go out.

> [*Leads her out, and turns to* KATHARINE.

And now, my little duck, don't flounce and pout.
You will be twice as happy, you will find,
When to "obey" you have made up your mind.

[*To Queen's Counsellor.*] And now, good sir, if you don't go
    off quick,
I'll haste your exit with a gentle kick.

KATHARINE.

My mother's Counsellor!   How dare you, sir!
I won't allow the Counsellor to stir.
Stay by me here, good friend, I pray.

QUEEN'S COUNSELLOR.

I know not which to do—to go or stay.

KATHARINE.

Stay, if you love me.

PETER SIMPLE.

                    Love me! what's that you said?
Perhaps you wish this ancient bird to wed.

KATHARINE.

Wed him! oh, never! though I vow 'tis true,
I love him better than I'll e'er love you.

PETER SIMPLE.

Comparisons are odorous, my sweet Kate;
But yet to mend it never is too late.
Before the ancient mariner sets sail,
I'll ask some questions which may now avail.
Answer me every word by yes and no,
Or, though a lady, Miss, to jail you'll go.
First, did you tell your love to him?   Eh?—Well

KATHARINE.

I never told my love—I'd none to tell.

PETER SIMPLE.

That is no answer.   Did he e'er love you?

KATHARINE.

I have no doubt he did.

QUEEN'S COUNSELLOR.

It is not true.

PETER SIMPLE.

Did you e'er think of love, e'en in your dreams?

KATHARINE.

You think my thoughts belong to you, it seems.

PETER SIMPLE.

Your thoughts before you think them I must know,
And hear them, too.   Answer me—yes or no.

KATHARINE.

I am a Princess, sir; I'm not afraid:
And love is privileged to every maid.

PETER SIMPLE.

Who cares for privilege, when on my side
I have the certainty you'll be my bride?
Is it not so, old brick? you ought to know.

QUEEN'S COUNSELLOR.

It don't look like it, friend.

PETER SIMPLE.

Away you go.
[*Exit* QUEEN'S COUNSELLOR *with a kick.*

Now, pretty darling, come, I'll sit beside you.

KATHARINE.

I'll tell you, sir, the truth—I can't abide you.

PETER SIMPLE.

Do you know, I really think I'm getting thinner:
What do you say, love, to our having dinner?

KATHARINE.

Dinner ! A man in love to think of eating !

PETER SIMPLE.

I'd like a beefsteak better than a sweet thing.
Get it at once ; I am not fond of waiting ;
And while I'm eating you can go on prating.

KATHARINE.

I'll see you further first, and then I won't.

PETER SIMPLE.

For this sweet speech I'll pay you.

[*Kisses her.*

KATHARINE.

Oh, sir, don't !

PETER SIMPLE.

Oh, yes, I will ; I am an honest man,
And pay for all I get the least I can.

KATHARINE.

In such base coin my debts shall not be paid.

PETER SIMPLE.

Go, get my dinner quick, you saucy jade.

KATHARINE.

Then it shan't be, and there's an end of it.

PETER SIMPLE.

Then it shall be, and you I'll send for it.

KATHARINE (*aside*).

What shall I do ?   I'm growing quite afraid ;
He seems to take me for the waiting maid.
I know what I will do, I'll hold my tongue,
And I'll not answer, though my neck were wrung.

[*Folds her arms, and stands quite still.*

PETER SIMPLE.

Katharine ! Dost hear me, pretty Mistress Kate?
Don't hurry, darling, I have time to wait.
She does not answer, she is in a pout.
I think I know a way to draw her out.

[*Sings.*

A wife, a spaniel, and a walnut-tree,
The more you beat them, the better they'll be.

[*Catches hold of* KATHARINE, *and flourishes his sword over
her head, singing " Voici le sabre de mon père."*

KATHARINE.

Oh, mercy, mercy! don't, oh don't do so :
I'll get your dinner if you'll let me go.

PETER SIMPLE.

No, no, you'd not come back ; I know you well,
So, by your leave, just go and ring the bell.

[KATHARINE *rings the bell.* MINNA *enters, and kneels
at her feet.*

PETER SIMPLE.

Get up, my girl ; no need to bow and scrape.
Get up, I say ! I'll take you by the nape.

KATHARINE.

Pray let her go, she is a willing maid.

PETER SIMPLE.

I don't care what she is, the saucy jade.

KATHARINE.

Go down, poor girl, and on the larder shelf
You'll find some mutton on a dish of delf ;
'Tis a cold shoulder, which will suit the Prince ;
And as for me, I'd like a little mince.

PETER SIMPLE.

Mincemeat I'll make of you, if you don't haste.

KATHARINE.

Bring me a *vol au vent* of lightest paste.

[*Exit* MINNA.

PETER SIMPLE.

And so you're hungry, too—come, that is good ;
But you shan't eat till I have had my food.

Re-enter MINNA *with a dish, on which is a bare bladebone.*

PETER SIMPLE.

And is this all your royal larder boasts ?
Is this the way your cook sends up her roasts ?
Now in your kitchen pride shall have a fall.
There—take it to you—trencher, cups, and all.

[PETER *kicks* MINNA, *tray and all, out.*

KATHARINE.

Oh, Crœsus, let me humbly intercede ;
To be in such a passion there's no need.

PETER SIMPLE.

I will be in a passion ; I don't care.
I'll stamp and rage ; I'll tear you by the hair.

[PETER *pulls off* KATHARINE'S *chignon.*

Hallo ! what's this ?   Your head has come in twain

KATHARINE.

Oh, give it back ; I'll pin it on again.
I know I am—I feel I'm going to faint.

[*Faints.*

PETER SIMPLE.

Red as a rose is she : I see the paint.
[*To Katharine.*] I am disgusted with your tricks of art ;
Such made-up charms can never win my heart.
I'll leave this palace, and return no more,
And seek a bride upon another shore.

I

KATHARINE.

Now I have lost him by my silly ways ;
The Prince I've dreamed of for so many days.
Oh, this will never do, my heart would break.
I feel I love him, though he's such a rake.

[PETER *turns his back on her, and stands quite still.*

Just see, he's turned on me his lovely back.
My tenderest feelings now are on the rack.
I never knew before I had a heart,
But now I feel the stab of Cupid's dart.
Crœsus ! I'll call him till he turns again.
Prince Crœsus ! all my words are vain.

[*Sings to the air of " Clochette."*

Silent is now Prince Crœsus.
    Grieved in my heart am I ;
For, though a sad coquette,
    For him I would gladly die.
Prince Crœsus ! Prince Crœsus !
    I'll die for love of thee.
Oh turn, then, dear Prince Crœsus ;
    Turn once again to me.

Hear me once more, Prince Crœsus :
    You must my true love take ;
Although a sad coquette,
    My heart will surely break.
Prince Crœsus ! Prince Crœsus !
    I know we'll happy be.
Prince Crœsus ! Prince Crœsus !
    Oh, say that you love me !

Crœsus, dost hear me ?

PETER SIMPLE.

No, I don't, I don't.

KATHARINE.

Crœsus, you'll love me ?

PETER SIMPLE.

No, I won't, I won't.

KATHARINE.

Oh yes, you shall.

PETER SIMPLE.

I tell you that I shan't.

KATHARINE.

Oh yes, you can.

PETER SIMPLE.

I tell you that I can't.

KATHARINE.

Turn, love, again your face so sunny.

PETER SIMPLE.

I know you only love me for my money.

KATHARINE.

I do not care a straw for all your pelf,
I only love you for your own sweet self.

PETER SIMPLE.

Now that's most kind of you, if 'twere but true.

KATHARINE.

Give me, I pray, a way to prove it you.

PETER SIMPLE (*aside*).

Now shall I risk my chance—the time is rife,
Either to win or lose a pretty wife.
[*Aloud.*] And so you love me ?

KATHARINE.

Yes, indeed, my Prince.
[PETER *shudders.*
Why should my words have caused that painful wince ?

PETER SIMPLE.

And so you love me?

KATHARINE.

Yes, with all my heart.
Never I'll ask again from you to part.

PETER SIMPLE.

And so you love me?

KATHARINE.

Yes, till death I'm thine.
Now let me in my arms my love entwine.

PETER SIMPLE.

And would you love me were I very poor?

KATHARINE.

I'd only love you, Crœsus, more and more.

PETER SIMPLE.

And if my name were " Peter," would it my love defeat?

KATHARINE.

A rose by any other name would smell as sweet.

PETER SIMPLE.

And if my mother were a hideous hag?

KATHARINE.

I'd love her, Crœsus, and I'd be her fag.

PETER SIMPLE.

And if my mother bid you bind your hair?

KATHARINE.

My chignon from my head I'd instant tear.

PETER SIMPLE.

And if my mother bid you dress quite plain?

KATHARINE.

I'd do it, love, and twice as much again.

PETER SIMPLE.

And for a peasant would you leave your home ?

KATHARINE.

With you the peasant, o'er the world I'd roam.

PETER SIMPLE.

Would you your father leave for love of me ?

KATHARINE.

I would forsake him for the love of thee.

PETER SIMPLE.

No further, dearest, need we now delay :
First let us kiss, and then we'll name the day.

[*Exeunt.*

END OF ACT IV.

ACT V.—*Woodland Scene.*

Enter WITCH *with a broomstick, dancing to the tune of " Can anyone
tell me where Peter's gone?"*

WITCH (*sings*)
Can anyone tell me where Peter's gone ?
Oh, how could he be so unkind ?

[*Dances.*

I once was so happy, but now I'm sad,
Oh, so sad—dreadfully sad,
Since Peter Simple behaved so bad :
Oh ! how could he be so unkind ?

[*Dances.*

(Speaks.)

Oh, I am lost, forlorn, destroyed, betrayed ;
I am outwitted by a silly maid.
Peter is not my Peter—not my son.
The Princess Delia has been wooed and won
By a false Prince, who, coming in disguise,
Courted the maiden 'fore my very eyes.
In Peter's dress, in Peter's hose he came,
And I, poor woman, helped his little game.
Now all is lost : the King 'gainst me will rage ;
Hang me, perhaps, or put me in a cage,
Or torture me with rack or cruel pain,
For Delia's beauty has returned again.
This morning, when I sought her at my place,
I found the spell had passed from off her face.
Surely the Prince must have a rare love given,
That my black arts should be asunder riven.
Hush ! in the wood I can some footsteps hear.
Who are this couple that are drawing near ?

[*Enter* PETER *and* KATHARINE.

Peter ! oh, Peter, Peter ! my dear boy !
So you've come back at last to be my joy.
And who's this little lady at your side ?

PETER SIMPLE.

This little lady is your Peter's bride.
She's a very nice girl, and as meek as a mouse ;
She'll polish your boots, and tidy your house.

WITCH.

She does not look like it in that gay dress ;
She'll polish herself, if I rightly guess.
A lady in flounces and frizzled hair
Will never put up with old Stycorax' lair.

KATHARINE.

I'll change this dress the moment I get home,
Nor ever from your cave will care to roam.
I care not now for silks or satin shoon ;
I'd rather be a cat and lick the spoon,
Than give up Peter.

WITCH.

All that's very fine.
Wait till at home on roasted frogs we dine.

KATHARINE.

I'd live on earwigs, if he liked it too.

WITCH.

You don't look like it, Mistress Cockatoo.

PETER SIMPLE.

There, little Kitty, give the dame a kiss ;
She won't be happy till you've given her this.

[KATHARINE *kisses* WITCH.

WITCH.

Well, come, she's not so bad ; I'll take her part.
She kissed my ugly face with all her heart.

KATHARINE.

I have kissed her, Peter ; what shall I do now?

PETER SIMPLE.

I'd like to see the dear old home, I vow ;
So trundle on, and we will jolly be.
Kitty, put the kettle on, we'll all have tea.

[*Exeunt,* PETER *singing* " *Home, sweet home,*"
merging into " *Kitty, put the kettle on.*"

Enter PRINCESS DELIA, *in her fine dress and without the mask.*

DELIA.

Now in this wood Prince Crœsus I should meet ;
But love has lent such wings unto my feet,

I have outrun my love. He is not here,
And I am now possessed with sudden fear ;
For since I woke this morn and found me changed,
A thousand doubts have through my bosom ranged.
He loved me as I was, a graceless maid,
Nor at my ugly face was he dismayed ;
His noble heart pitied my hapless plight,
And only more endeared me in his sight.
I had no wish my beauty to regain ;
I know I'm pretty now—though I'm not vain.
But should my change of face cause change of heart,
From all my beauty would I gladly part ;
Again I'd hie me to old Stycorax' den,
If only he would love me now as then.
I loved him when I thought him Simple Peter,
Nor will a Prince's dress now make him sweeter.
But will he love me in my change of dress,
And all his wealth of love to me confess ?
Hush ! here he comes. Now, beating heart, keep still ;
I soon shall know whether he loves me still.

Enter PRINCE CRŒSUS *in his own dress.*

PRINCE CRŒSUS.

Here Delia vowed she'd keep her faithful tryst,
And yet among the trees her form I've missed.
Should Delia as a Prince my love disdain,
I never in this world could love again.

[*Perceives* DELIA.

Ah, here's a lovely maid in silver sheen :
I'll ask her if my Delia she has seen.
Prythee, fair maid, did you, in wand'ring nigh,
See a poor maiden who was passing by ?

DELIA.

What was she like ? and was she passing fair ?
What kind of eyes had she ? what kind of hair ?

PRINCE CRŒSUS.

I know not how she'd strike a passer-by ;
I in her face nothing but charms descry.

DELIA.

Then no ! she was not here.   I saw a maid,
But with a face so plain, I was afraid.

PRINCE CRŒSUS.

You need not so have feared, nor shunned her eyes ;
She is an angel in a girl's disguise.

DELIA (*aside.*)

Oh, how he loved me—but my heart doth tremble :
Yet once again with him I must dissemble.
[*Aloud.*] I too am wandering in this wood in vain,
For one who promised me to come again.
Did you, perchance, abroad *my* lover see ?—
A youth as stately as a poplar tree ;
With crimson cloak and green and golden hose ;
With eyes that read my thoughts, and Roman nose ;
With lips that ever his true love asserted.

PRINCE CRŒSUS.

I saw him not.

DELIA.

Ah, then I am deserted !

PRINCE CRŒSUS.

Sweet maiden, dry your tears, they are but vain ;
No one who loved thee once could love again.

DELIA.

Ah ! say you so ? [*Aside.*] Now will I test his truth.
[*Aloud.*] And could'st thou love me, thinkest thou, forsooth ?

PRINCE CRŒSUS.

Madam, the question somewhat takes me back.

DELIA.

Then you won't love me—oh, alack! alack!

PRINCE CRŒSUS.

Ah, the poor maid, her pretty head is turned,
Since by her faithless lover she is spurned.
Had I been he, I would have prized my choice;
For she has Delia's ways and Delia's voice.

DELIA.

Away he turns his face—what doth he say?
Oh listen, gentle youth, I humbly pray.
If you will take me for your own true wife,
I will most faithful be for all my life;
And I will love you with a love so rare,
All other love will perish in despair.
I will divine your thoughts, your sorrows soothe;
The thorns I'll pluck away; your path make smooth.
Say that you'll love me—pity my despair.

PRINCE CRŒSUS.

I must not listen to your words, my fair.
If that of broken vows you feel the smart,
Why would you seek to break another heart?
Delia alone to me is prized and fair,
And she alone shall all my true love share.
Now from this wood I will at once depart,
Where I can nothing say to soothe her heart.

[PRINCE *turns away.* DELIA *follows him and sings
to the tune of* "*I built a bridge of fancies.*"

Oh don't you know me, Crœsus?
I'm your Delia fond and true,

Who in the witch's cottage
    You fondly sought to woo.
How oft you asked with longing
    That I would grant one kiss;
But now you turn with a shudder,
    And seek for no such bliss.

Oh, turn once more, Prince Crœsus,
    And look into my face;
Am I so much less worthy
    To feel your kind embrace?
'Tis true the mask has fallen,
    That once did hide these eyes;
But now that you see their softness,
    You cannot them despise.

PRINCE CRŒSUS.

That is my Delia's voice—it must be true;
And are you Delia that I once did woo?
How 'neath this mask could I these charms divine?

DELIA.

Pardon my blushes—I am Delia—thine.
I am your Delia, changed in face alone,
For all my heart and love are still your own.

PRINCE CRŒSUS.

O pearl most rare, just issued from thy shell,
The love I thought so great doth higher swell;
E'en as I gaze this love doth grow to bliss.
Come, let us seal it with one loving kiss.

DELIA.

Hush! I hear steps; some one is drawing near:
It is my father; it is King De Lear.
Here let us hide a moment, 'neath the trees,
That I may crave his love upon my knees.

Enter KING DE LEAR, *mad, and fantastically dressed up with flowers.*

KING.

Blow winds and crack your cheeks till they do weep ;
Rumble thy inside full, so full of grief.
Where is my Delia flown—my gentle dove,
She who did cherish me with tender love ?
Katharine, who vowed that no love could us part,
Has broken, for a beggar's sake, my heart ;
She who did call me her life and her joy,
Has left King De Lear for the broth of a boy.
Oh, cats, dogs, and vipers, and little fat mice,
Now hearken to me for a word of advice :
Never trust in a woman, however so fair ;
She will drive you to ruin, if not to despair.
Oh, waves of the heavens and clouds of the sea,
Can none of you tell me where Delia can be ?
But off with my boots, for bootless are tears :
Rain, wind, thunder, fire—I'll box all your ears.
Not one pitying eye doth my misery scan ;
I am a poor despised, infirm old man.

[*Sinks down at the foot of a tree.*

Enter QUEEN, *weeping, and* QUEEN'S COUNSELLOR.

QUEEN.

Where is my hushand gone, once so imperious ?
Lordly De Lear is now poor King De Lirious.
And where are my daughters ?   Alas and alack !
They both have gone off, and they'll never come back :
And all the sweet mirth from my heart hath departed,
Since I from my daughters and hushand was parted.

[*Sings.*

I cannot sing the old songs
    I sang long years ago,
For heart and voice would fail me,
    And foolish tears would flow.

Ah, here's my husband, sitting on the ground.
My poor old man, and is it thus you're found?

QUEEN'S COUNSELLOR.

Take him up gingerly, lift him with care,
Fashioned so brittle-ly, marked " Glass with care."

KING.

Where am I now? Where art thou, fair daylight?
You did me wrong to wake me in the night;
I might have slept this hideous dream away.

QUEEN'S COUNSELLOR.

Sir, we are in the wood, and it is day.

KING.

And who are you, and have you Delia seen?

QUEEN.

I am your wife—your poor unhappy Queen. [*Weeps.*]

KING.

Could you not Delia call to dry my eyes?

QUEEN'S COUNSELLOR.

His tears do fall like water from the skies.

KING.

Aye, I will call her, though I know 'tis vain.
Delia, oh Delia! come to us again.

DELIA *enters and throws her arms round him.*

DELIA.

Father, dear father! and my mother kind!

KING.

Do I my daughter see, or am I blind?

QUEEN.

Alas! Alack! did not I tell you so?
Rage, Sorrow, Vengeance, Pain—four words of woe!
Is this our Delia fair?   Now must I weep.

DELIA.

Mother, your tears give o'er, your sorrow keep.

KING.

Oh, my sweet Delia! Oh, my darling child!
My fears for thee had almost driven me wild.
I do repent me of the foul design
Which robbed me for a time of love like thine.
Forgive me, child!

DELIA.

My dearest father, cease.
Let's all forgive, and then there will be peace.
I have a boon to crave from you as well,
And here is one who will the secret tell.
Here is Prince Crœsus, who my hand hath won.
Take him, dear father, for your loving son.

KING.

Can I my eyes believe?   Is this Prince Crœsus,
Knight of the Red Cross Band and Golden Fleeces?

PRINCE CRŒSUS.

Aye, Sire, and at your hand I humbly crave
The right to live for aye her willing slave.

KING.

Rise up, Prince Crœsus; rise, my friend, and know
You've lifted from my heart a load of woe.
Take her from me for better or for worse,
And with her also take my realm and purse.

PRINCE CRŒSUS.

Nay, I want nothing but her own sweet self ;
And give to Princess Kate your hoarded wealth.

KING.

I will not hear of her : speak not her name ;
She has humbled my pride, and sullied my fame.
She loved me not, although her love she vowed,
In hopes the match with you would be allowed.
But now she's found her match in Stycorax' son,
I'll let her finish what she has begun.
I'll not forgive her till she loves like you,
And gives for nothing love that is my due.

QUEEN'S COUNSELLOR.

Great Sire, I have a message for the King,
And must an answer to the suppliants bring.
A country youth and a poor humble maid
Are waiting here to see you in the shade.

KING.

Bid them come in, for in our new-found joys,
All are most welcome, be they girls or boys.

QUEEN'S COUNSELLOR.

Nay, here they are—impatient of delay,
Their eager footsteps could no longer stay.

Enter KATHARINE, *plainly dressed ; she kneels to the* KING.

KATHARINE.

Pity the sorrows of a poor young thing,
Whose trembling limbs now kneel before the King.
I had a father once, who loved me well,
More than my lips can speak, or tongue can tell :

He was a kind old man—his hair was grey—
Not one harsh word e'er did I hear him say ;
And yet I left him, like a heartless maid,
And all his tender love most ill repaid.

KING.

That was not right—it was not right, my child.

KATHARINE.

And what was worse, my folly drove him wild.
I left him for a lover, poor, but true,
Whose purse was empty, and whose charms were few.
Nor of my choice do I e'en now repent,
Were but a message from my father sent,
To say he'd love me, and would still forgive,
And let me in his favour always live.
No happiness in life can I attain,
Until he loves and blesses me again.

KING.

Would that my Katharine thus with me might plead.
Gladly, my girl, for thee I'll intercede.
Who is your father ?

KATHARINE.

You, oh, you, my King !

QUEEN.

Now is not this a most surprising thing ?
And so that's Katharine in that wretched gown ? [*Weeps.*]

DELIA.

Mother, your tears just for this once keep down.

KING.

And so you are my child, my life, my lamb !
And where is Peter Simple ?

PETER enters.

PETER SIMPLE.

Here I am !
And hope, old boy, that you and I'll be friends.

KING.

All's well, great Shakespeare says, that haply ends ;
So I'll forgive, and by and by forget,
As upon peace our royal heart is set.

PETER SIMPLE.

Well, now, as we are friends with one another,
Suppose I go and fetch my poor old mother.

[*Exit* PETER.

KING.

One touch of kindness makes the whole world kin,
And he who loves his mother 's sure to win.
My kingdom in two halves I will divide,
And give a portion to each happy bride.

Re-enter PETER *and* WITCH.

PETER SIMPLE.

Here is my mother, and I humbly pray
You'll give the dear old soul her little say.
She has a moral hidden in her sleeve,
Which she will give you now, with your kind leave.

WITCH.

My moral 's neither wearisome nor long,
But while I con it o'er let's have song.

SONG, *to be sung by* PRINCE CRŒSUS, *to the air of* " *Polly Perkins*." *Chorus by all the characters, who take hands and dance round at the end of each verse.*

His Majesty, the King, most eccentric and old,
Who pocketed the tinsel, and threw away the gold ;
'Tis very hard to determine whether he was more wise
Before he lost his little senses, or after their demise.

K

Here's our good Queen Lackadaisical, whose tears never stay—
Oh, the numberless pocket-handkerchiefs she damps in a day !
Hysterics are her exercise, and groans her delight,
And you hear her sounding her fog-signals—from morning till night.

Here's Kate, a bright example, but yet I'm afraid
You cannot trust the roadster, who once was a jade ;
With her love-making and bread-baking, the very first check,
She may hoist and throw brave Peter clean over her neck.

From her chrysalis, gentle Delia now shines forth again,
Who proved herself irresistible when amiable and plain ;
Her pleading eyes solicit you, and ask if you would
Just offer her some small encouragement—now she's beautiful and
       good.

The buxom little maiden, so brisk at her task,
Who is waiting here to marry if there's anyone to ask ;
Cheer up, my little spinster, and make no advance ;
Just purr in patience in your corner, and—you'll have your chance.

Here's Stycorax, old witch, with spell, ban, and hubbub,
Who has one little touch of nature, her love for her cub;
If she cast on you her evil eye, a mischief it bodes—
Oh ! look away, my pretty ladies, or she'll change you to toads.

The Counsellor ! the Counsellor ! so burly and big,
The thoughts they come clustering on the eaves of his wig ;
Most imperious, most impressive, a person of brains,
The King's his most obedient subject—'tis the Counsellor who reigns.

His Royal Highness, " Peter," so rude and so bold,
How very like the donkey with the pannier of gold.
Peter, oh ! bully Peter, I wouldn't be you ;
   Tis a stone that's always rolling down again, is " the taming of a
      shrew."

Two pages of small consequence must now have a word ;
They have just comprehended one-half that occurred ;
But let them see you do like this [*Clap*], and when you begin,
You'll see the jolly little pixies, how brightly they'll grin.

Your usher now I've acted, and here in my turn,
Upon my performance your verdict I'd learn ;
But even if a " failure," strict justice demands,
Lest you should wound my pretty Princess, pray give me your
   hands.

WITCH.

Old folks and young folks, when they're able,
Skip with consent the moral of the fable.
The moral of our play can never pall,
While love, true love, still holds the world in thrall ;
Love for a father, mother, husband, friend,
This is a moral that can never end.
And as it has no end, no longer we'll delay,
But ask your kind applause for this our little play.

[*Curtain falls*

END OF " PRINCE CRŒSUS."

NETTLE COATS;

OR,

THE SILENT PRINCESS.

BY

THE HON.ᴮᴸᴱ· MRS. GREENE AND F. M. S.

(Adapted partly from the German of HANS ANDERSEN.)

DRAMATIS PERSONÆ.

PRINCE NOBLEHEART.

LORD CHAMBERLAIN TO THE PRINCE.

PRINCE HUGH,
PRINCE JACK,
PRINCE WILL,
PRINCE JOE,
PRINCE JAMES,
PRINCE HARRY,

Six young Princes, brothers to the Princess Nellie.

EXECUTIONER.

QUEEN SNAP-EM-UP (*stepmother to the six Princes and Nellie*).

PRINCESS NELLIE (*sister to the six Princes*).

WITCH WORTHY.

DRESS.

PRINCE NOBLEHEART.—Blue velvet cap, bordered with swansdown, and a plume of white feathers; blue velvet tunic and knickerbockers, slashed with white, and trimmed round the slashings with gold and red braid; white silk stockings; blue shoes, with gold rosettes; scarlet cloak (not large), and trimmed with ermine and gold braid.

LORD CHAMBERLAIN.—Old-fashioned Court suit, with tights; black silk stockings and lace ruffles; *large* gold eye-glass and chain; steel buttons and lace ruffles to breast of coat and sleeves; black shoes and steel buckles; *large* cockle hat.

SIX PRINCES all dressed alike in suits of black velvet, slashed with yellow, and trimmed with red and gold braid; gold crowns and long flaxen wigs; scarlet stockings, and black shoes, with yellow rosettes.

SIX PRINCES (*as Storks*).—The breast and neck and head of Storks can be formed of light basket-work or papier-maché, fitting over the head and round the waist of the wearer; holes must be left in basket-work for the arms, and the basket-work representing stork's breast must be bowed out very considerably, so as to admit the wearer's head, and also very lightly woven, so as wearer may breathe and see through the interstices.

The neck and head of storks should be covered either with swansdown or white glazed calico; very large eyes, made of yellow glazed calico, with a large black centre.

A dress of white calico, combining shirt and knickerbockers (all in one), should be fastened round the lower part of stork's neck, and joining hidden by ruff of swansdown. This dress must be entirely covered over with newspapers, cut and painted so as to resemble feathers; newspaper wings painted in like manner must be attached to the arms; very coarse painting on newspaper, done with common blacking, will make a capital representation of feathers.

Scarlet stockings, which should be drawn over shoes.

EXECUTIONER.—Long black dress, and black mask covering half the face.

QUEEN SNAP-EM-UP.—Black dress, with low body and short sleeves; large white ruff; long yellow train, ornamented with grotesque figures in black velvet; white wig; crown; and large hooked false nose and spectacles; sceptre.

PRINCESS NELLIE.—Dolly Varden upper skirt, over a green silk petticoat (short); white stockings and green shoes, with rosettes; Dolly Varden cap trimmed to match.

PRINCESS NELLIE (*second*): WEDDING DRESS.—White dress (long) and veil covered with silver spangles; tiara of diamonds.

WITCH WORTHY.—Pointed black hat, covered with scarlet symbols and demons, cut out of tinsel paper; scarlet petticoat and black velvet cloak, also adorned with emblematical figures and signs; high-heeled shoes and steel buckles; broomstick.

NETTLE COATS;

OR,

THE SILENT PRINCESS.

ACT I.—*Children's Meal in the Palace.*

PRINCESS NELLIE *setting six chairs round the table.*

PRINCESS NELLIE.

Alas, my poor brothers! each day they grow thinner;
And how can one wonder, with this for their dinner?

> [*Points to table.*

Dry crusts and a cabbage—no turkey or ham:
I remember the time we got pudding and jam!
But the good days are past, and the bad days are come,
Since Queen Snap-em-up reigns in our once happy home.
Oh, why is our father so long at the wars?
Will he leave us to die in our stepmother's claws?
Poor Jack, Hugh, and Harry; Will, Joey, and James—
Such dear little fellows—*she* calls them bad names.
She pulls their sweet noses, and boxes their ears,
Till their dear little eyes are all brimming with tears.
And I may not help them, nor for mercy may cry;
Tho' to save them such torment I'd willingly die.

Enter PRINCE JACK, *and sits down.*

PRINCE JACK.

My dear sister Nellie, I'm in great perturbation ;
There has come to my ears a most strange revelation.
I will make you recipient of all I have heard,
The minutest particulars which have occurred.
For the truth of the story I cannot well answer ;
But 'tis rumoured the Queen is a dark necromancer.

PRINCESS NELLIE.

Necromancer ! dear brother, pray what does that mean ?

PRINCE JACK.

You're the stupidest girl that I ever have seen.
On each word that I say you request information ;
I suppose I must give you the right derivation.
Necromancer's a word of a complex extraction,
From *negro*, a black man—that's proved to a fraction—
And *mancer*—why, surely a man is a man, sir !
That's as plain as a pike-staff ; and that is my answer.

PRINCESS NELLIE.

He's so dreadfully wise, and so full of his learning ;
His words are so long, they are past my discerning.

PRINCE JACK.

She practises arts of the darkest astrology,
And could change us to beasts by Electro-Biology !

PRINCESS NELLIE.

To beasts !—but oh, hush ! for here comes the others.
'Twere cruel to frighten our dear little brothers.

Enter four Princes, who seat themselves on four chairs round the table.

PRINCE JOE.

Oh, dear, I'm so hungry ! Miss Nellie, I pray,
Is there anything good for our dinner to-day ?

PRINCESS NELLIE.

Six crusts and a cabbage, some water and salt ;
Indeed, my dear brothers, it is not *my* fault.
I begged for some soup in the cabbage's place :
She gave me for answer a slap in my face.
I don't care for the pain, but I cry when I think
You've so little to eat and so little to drink.
But *one* chair is empty ! Where have you left Hugh ?
I thought he came into the parlour with you.

PRINCE JAMES.

I don't know where he is, for he stopped by the way ;
But I was too tired and hungry to stay.
To think *some* king's children should feed upon crust,
While other king's children may eat till they "bust."

PRINCE HUGH'S *voice heard outside the door :*

How do you like your potatoes done ?
Waxy, mealy, underdone ?
Hokey-pokey-winkey-wum—
I say, my boys, we'll have some fun.

Enter PRINCE HUGH, *carrying a steaming saucepan in his hand.*

PRINCE HUGH.

Oh, isn't this jolly ? See, boys, what I've got !
Some steaming potatoes, just fresh from the pot.
The cook in the kitchen—oh, was not she *waxy ?*
But away I skedaddled before she could catch me.
Here's one for each brother—the eldest comes "fust,"
[*Helps himself.*
Miss Nellie may eat up the cabbage and crust.

PRINCESS NELLIE.

Yes, Nellie may eat up the rubbish ! No matter ;
I'd live upon *stones*, if the boys would grow fatter.

PRINCE JOE.

I don't feel exactly as if I'd enough—
Is there nothing at all but potatoes to stuff?
I'd like a roast apple, plum-pudding, or quinces.

PRINCE HUGH.

But potatoes are quite good enough for *us* princes.
Our lady the *Queen* may have tartlets and pears;
While she has enough it is little she cares.

[Sings, to the air of " Not for Joe."

Her name is Great Queen Snap-up;
    Her foes they call her Snap.
She's up to every mortal thing,
    Can box, and pinch, and slap.
        No, no, no; not for Joe.
        Not for princes, tarts and quinces;
        No, no, no!

[Gong sounds outside.

Enter the QUEEN, *angrily.*

QUEEN.

Hey-day, young Princes, stop this row.
Why, what on earth has happened now?
You've over-eaten—that is clear.
What's in that jug?   I'm sure 'tis beer!

*[PRINCE JACK jumps up with a large potato in his mouth,
and looks into the jug.*

PRINCE JACK.

Yes, yes, your Grace, 'tis Adam's ale,
A trifle flat and *ex*-tra pale.

QUEEN.

Insolent youth!   Take that, and that!   *[Strikes him.]*
'Twill make your cheek a trifle flat.

PRINCESS NELLIE *(springing forward).*

Spare him, your Majesty! oh, spare!
Poor Jack is choking!   Please take care.

PRINCE JAMES (*running towards Jack*).

That's *my* potato—give it back.
You've eaten yours, you greedy Jack,
And taken mine.

QUEEN.

What's that you say?
Potatoes! I ordered none to-day.
So you've been stealing—shameful boys.
This was the cause of all the noise.
No more of this—the time is past ;
Your punishment is come at last.
No longer in this house you'll stay.
Now listen to the words I say :
I have a power—a fearful power,
Which you shall feel this selfsame hour.
With but a word, with but a wish,
You straight are changed to bird or fish.
Miss Nellie here may make the choice,
For none of you shall have a voice.

PRINCE JAMES, *coming forward, sings in a dolorous voice :*

I would I were a bird,
If I might be a flower ;
But really, on my word,
She cannot have this power.

PRINCE HUGH, *coming forward, in a still more dolorous voice sings
to the air of " Nelly Bly."*

I'd like to be a lively flea,
Hopping where I goes ;
I'd like to jump on Queen Snap-up,
And bite her on the nose.

[*Points to the* QUEEN'S *long nose. All the
Princes burst out laughing.*

QUEEN (*very angrily*).

Cease your funning.   Speak, I say,
Nor turn my solemn spell to play.

PRINCESS NELLIE.

Before your Majesty I kneel,
To make one piteous, last appeal.
Unsay those cruel words you said.
I am a useless little maid;
I have no beauty, and no grace;
I have an ugly little face.
Oh, drive *me* forth alone to roam;
No one will miss me from my home.

QUEEN.

Come, cease your prating, foolish dunce,
For you *shall* choose, and choose *at once*.

PRINCESS NELLIE.

Then must I choose—oh, luckless day,
That drives my brothers far away!
Hast thou no pity in thy heart,
To force on *me* this cruel part?

QUEEN.

Pity! I know not what it means.
Pity may do for girls in teens;
For love to pity is allied,
And *both* long since in me have died.

PRINCESS NELLIE.

No longer can I now refuse
Between a bird or fish to choose.
Were Jack a crow, or James an ee
I know some cruel pain they'd feel.

For birds are shot, and fish are caught,
And both are eaten !—horrid thought !
I could not bear my own sweet Will
To feel a hook within his gill,
Or Armstrong gun to plant a smart
Within my Joey's loving heart.
[*Aside.*] Stay ! stay ! a thought my bosom thrills :
There *is* a bird that no man kills—
The sacred Stork, which builds its nest
Above the homes wherein we rest.
I'll give no reason for my choice.
[*Aloud.*] Great Queen, now deign to hear my voice :
If that you have this power strange,
My brothers six to birds to change,
Make them, not cruel kites or hawks,
But change them into " patient Storks."

QUEEN.

To Storks ! Well, yes, they're ugly creatures,
With long red shanks and sharpened features.
Your words have sense ; your choice is sound ;
For uglier birds could scarce be found.

PRINCE HUGH (*shaking his hand angrily at Nellie*).
A Stork ! was that the bird you chose,
With such a hideous, ugly nose ?
                    [*Points at the* QUEEN's *nose, and retires.*

PRINCE JACK (*also angrily at Nellie*).
You meddling magpie, with your chatter,
You've put your foot into this matter.
While you can feather your own nest,
You little care what suits us best.
You think you've paid me out with skill—
Wait till you meet my fine long bill.

QUEEN.

Boys, cease; I know what I'm about.
You *shall* be Storks.   And now STALK out.

[*Exit Princes.*

QUEEN (*to Nellie*).

And if *you* dare your father tell,
I'll change you to a Stork as well.
'Tis but for *this* your life I save—
To keep you for my patient slave.

[*Exit* QUEEN.

PRINCESS NELLIE (*alone*).

The last link is broken which binds me to home,
For over this bleak world my brothers must roam ;
For the winter is coming, and over the sea
They must fly from this land and their home and from me.
Is there no way to help them ?   Is there no way to save ?

[*Pauses to think.*

I will hie me *at once* to the good Witches' Cave.

END OF ACT I.

ACT II.—*The Witches' Cave.   Thunder rolls in the distance, and
lightning flashes.*

Enter PRINCESS NELLIE *without shoes ; her hair all blown about, and her hat
hanging over her shoulder.   She looks anxiously about, and starts at the
flashes of lightning.   She advances to the front.*

Six days and six nights I have wandered alone,
Thro' a land where my name and my face are unknown.
My heart beats so wildly—I feel a strange fear ;
Ah ! here is the Cave.   If I knock, will she hear ?

[*Knocks.   Thunder rolls loud and long, and no one answers.*

I wonder what all this delay is about.
No answer !   Oh, what shall I do if she's out ?

[*Knocks again ; loud peals of thunder.*

Witch Worthy, now are you within doors, I pray ?
To consult you I've come such a very long way.
You promised my mother her babes to befriend,
And if anyone hurt us, that you would defend.
Are you in ?

[Knocks again. Thunder and red fire.

WITCH WORTHY'S *voice is heard from the cave.*

Who goes there—a friend or a foe ?
For the sound of the voice is not one that I know.

[Comes out of the cave.

Eh ! eh ! little damsel, so wan and so pale,
What brings thee so late to this desolate vale ?
Hast no fear of the bears or the wolves that do prowl
The cry of the vulture, the screech of the owl ?
Few maidens so young and so tender as thee,
Would venture to visit an old hag like *me.*

PRINCESS NELLIE.

I'm Nellie : I've come such a number of miles ;
I've waded through rivers and climbed over stiles.

WITCH.

And *stylish* she looks in her present array ;
But go on, little maiden, I hear what you say.

PRINCESS NELLIE.

My hands are all bleeding ; my feet are all torn ;
For I lost the new boots I had only once worn.

WITCH.

But *bootless* no longer your journey shall be,
For you've come to the right shop in coming to me ;
For I'm a good *soul*, and to *heal* is my trade,
And the shoe never pinches, these fingers have made.

PRINCESS NELLIE.

Oh ! where are my brothers—now tell me, I pray—
My six little brothers who all flew away ?

L

WITCH.

Why, how can boys fly ?   Come, child, hasten your words.

PRINCESS NELLIE.

They all flew away, Ma'am, because they were birds.

WITCH.

But what kind of birds ?   Why, what nonsense she talks !

PRINCESS NELLIE.

Queen Snap-em-up changed them all six into Storks !

WITCH.

Queen Snap-em-up at her bad tricks once again !
I call that *foul* play.   Ah, the wicked old hen !
At the game " *Chicken Hazard*," *two* play, my sweet duck ;
And it is not the first crow with her I shall pluck.
She means to hatch treason, but *I'm* not afraid ;
Her eggs I will addle, although they're new-laid.
Her designs I'll break open ; her schemes I will baulk ;
I hold the true magic for changing a Stork !

PRINCESS NELLIE.

You know the true magic ?   Oh ! prithee, then, tell
If I can assist you in breaking the spell ?

WITCH.

Assist ?   Yes, a sister alone can assist ;
[*Aside.*] It rhymes like " a twister, a twisting a twist."
[*Aloud.*] You see, little maid, I can't help being witty,
Though my heart at the same time is brimful of pity :
So just listen to me, and a truce to all funning ;
We will talk in plain English, and give up our punning ;
For nothing, I tell you, your brothers can save,
But a heart that is loving and patient and brave.
Have you this, little maiden ?

PRINCESS NELLIE.
>   I love them so well,
I would give up my life, could that break through the spell.

WITCH (*taking Nellie by the hand*).

Come, show me your hand now, you poor little sister.
How sad it would be those white fingers to blister!
But oh! the dark nettles that grow in the shade—
Of these must six coats for your brothers be made.

PRINCESS NELLIE.

Of nettles! They'll sting me!

WITCH.
>   Aye, there comes the sting;
But have you not said you're a brave little thing?
And what will be worse, while these coats you are spinning,
Not a word must be said from the very beginning.
Till the last thread is woven, till the wheel stands at rest,
And in nettle-leaf coats your six brothers are dressed,
Not a word must be spoken—not so much as a breath!
Though they throw you in prison, or drag you to death!
When the last coat is finished, and not until then,
Your six spell-bound brothers will be changed back to m

PRINCESS NELLIE.

I will do it, Witch Worthy; I fear not the pain,
If only my brothers will come back again.

WITCH.

Well done, my brave child: when that happiness comes,
At Queen Snap-up herself we will all snap our thumbs.
>   [WITCH *moves towards the cave.*

PRINCESS NELLIE (*following her*).

But *where* are my brothers? May I see them once more?
Oh! I pray you, Witch Worthy, don't shut up your door!

WITCH *(turning round)*.

Hie away, little maiden, and do as you're bid ;
Shut the door of your mouth, and you'll never be chid.

[*Exit* WITCH.

NELLIE, *alone (advances to the front of the stage)*.

She is gone from my sight ; good Witch Worthy is gone,   .
And I in this dark wood must wander alone.
I must gather sharp nettles, and spin all the day,
And not one little word she'll allow me to say.
Indeed it will be a most difficult task—
All kind words to keep down, my feelings to mask.
What a terrible thought ! should I meet a dear brother,
To shut up my mouth, and my true love to smother !
Never mind ; when I've finished the six coats of leaves,
They will stretch out their wings and fly down from the eaves,
Then my tongue will be loosed, and my voice be set free :
And when once they are changed, oh ! I *know* they'll love me.
So at once to my work I will go with a will,
For although I mayn't speak, I may think of them still.

[*Exit* NELLIE.

END OF ACT II.

ACT III.—*Woodland Scene.*

Enter Stork.

PRINCE WILL.

Alack a day ! my wings are tired ;
My little strength is all expired.
We've flown so long, we've flown so far,
That now I wonder where we are.
If birds could weep, I'd pipe my eye,
That *bird's eye pipes* you can't deny.

My gentle audience, that's a joke,
A feeble pun that ends in smoke.
How can I joke at such a time,
A wanderer from my native clime,
From father, home, and little sister?
I did not think we could have missed her.

Enter PRINCE HUGH, *cheerfully singing to the air of " Cheer up, Sam."*

Cheer up, Storks; don't let your spirits go down;
There's many a snug warm chimney-top
Awaiting for us in the town.

Hey, Will, old fellow, what's the row?
What has been happening to you now?
Come, keep your pecker up, old lad;
You'll get no good by being sad.

*Enter the rest of the Storks, who arrange themselves in a semi-circle; flapping their
wings slowly, they begin to sing to the air " Slap, bang."*

Clap! clap! here we are again:
Here we are again; here we are again.
Clap! clap! here we are again :
What wretched old storks are we.

PRINCE HUGH.

Come listen, my brothers, to what has occurred,
And don't call me flighty, although I'm a bird.
Last night I flew home to the old palace gate,
And nobody saw me, because it was late.
I lit on the roof in a *suitable* spot,
And craned down the neck of a tall chimney-pot.
'Twas an awkward position; the chimney was high;
But I wanted our poor little sister to spy.

PRINCE HARRY.

And the view you were taking was strictly *bird's eye.*

PRINCE HUGH.

Shut up, you old stupid, and wait till I've done,
Or I'll *pun*ish you well for that villanous pun.
No Nellie I saw when I looked down the flue,
But my lady the Queen in a precious fine stew.
For our father was asking where all of us were ;
And when she didn't answer, he tugged at her hair.
I fancy, from something I heard father say,
The Queen has sent Nellie our sister away.
But loudly she pleaded, and loudly she swore,
She never put Nellie outside of the door.
Then the King would not list to a word more she said,
But tore in his fury the crown from her head.

Storks laugh wildly, and sing :

Clap, slap, give it her again ;
Give it her again ; give it her again.
Clap, slap, give it her again :
What a wretched old hag is she !

PRINCE HARRY.

But what about Nellie ? poor Nellie so kind ?

PRINCE HUGH.

We'll hunt all the country till Nellie we'll find.
Thy courage would mount, and my spirits recover,
If once we could find her and tell her we love her.

[NELLIE *here enters the stage, carrying a spinning-wheel in
one hand and a bunch of nettles in the other. After a
minute or two she perceives the Storks ; recognises them,
but cannot speak. Smiles as she hears* PRINCE HUGH's
words, and stoops to gather nettles.

PRINCE JACK.

I wish to hear more of your journey last night.
Was Queen Snap-em-up there in a precious good fright ?
Did she yell ?   Did she bawl ?   Did she flounce all about ?
Or bite all her nails, and sit down in a pout ?

PRINCE HUGH.

She bit more than her nails, for she flew to the kitchen,
And when she got there—if she didn't just pitch in !
She beat all the servants, upset all the kettles——
I say—who's that little girl gathering nettles ?

[All the Storks turn round in the direction of NELLIE.

PRINCE JACK.

Our own little Nellie, we thought far away.
Oh, Nellie ! we've searched for you many a day.

*[*NELLIE *stretches out her arms to them silently ;*
Storks gather round her.

PRINCE JOE.

Eh? Nellie, dear Nellie, pray why don't you speak ?

PRINCE JACK.

Or are you too angry, or tired, or weak ?

PRINCE HUGH.

Be quiet, you ganders, you're wasting your words.
Of course she don't know us, because we are birds.
We're a band of poor brothers, most beautiful Nell :
We were changed into Storks by a wicked Queen's spell.

*[*NELLIE *nods her head, and kisses each of the Storks in turn.*

PRINCE HUGH.

Come, Nellie, my girl, why don't you speak ?

[Puts her arms round PRINCE HUGH'S *long neck.*
The bunch of nettles touch him.

Hallo ! I say ! you've stung my beak.
Perhaps you think that *beaks* can't feel.
And what's the use of that spinning-wheel ?
Making coats out of nettles, as sure as a gun !

[Gun sounds in the distance.

That gun sounds too near us—I think we must run ;

For, though storks are held sacred, I very much fear
They soon would discover that you thought us *dear.*

                            [Exit Storks slowly, singing in chorus.

Quack ! quack ! we'll come back to you again !
We'll come back to you again ; we'll come back to you again.
Quack ! quack ! we'll come back to you again :
What good little Storks are we !"

Enter CHAMBERLAIN, *skipping forwards with an enormous eye-glass ; he looks about
in every direction for the bird which the* PRINCE *is supposed to have shot. Hurries
after the retreating Storks and beckons to them.*

CHAMBERLAIN.

Hey dey ! you come back here : I'll wager my head,
My master the Prince has shot some of you dead.
Come back ! don't you hear me ? for one of you fell.
Good luck ! here's a feather, the story to tell.

               [Takes up a feather off the ground and examines it through his eye-glass.

I'm right, 'tis a feather : I thought I was right—
I'm not often wrong,—'tis the quill of a Kite.

                                 [Looks at NELLIE.

Now, hearts, darts, and daggers, what have we got here,
All crouched in the nettles ? a pretty young dear.
See how she gathers them ; mark how she spins.
Her sighs, they go through me like needles and pins.
   feel somewhat queerish ; I've a most feeling heart,
And many's the time I have felt Cupid's dart.
It's rather a bore, for ofttimes in a flurry
I propose to a girl in too much of a hurry.
They accept me, of course, *cela va sans dire ;*
And when I won't have them, there's many a tear.
Now, before the Prince comes, I'll just steal to her side,
And ask the dear creature if she'll be my bride.
I feel somewhat bashful, but I must be plucky ;
So now or never. Oh, you duckey !

[Rushes towards her, and sings, to the air of "Pretty Jemima, don't say No:"

> Pretty little maiden, don't say No !
> Oh, hi ! ho !
> Pretty little maiden, don't say No !
> And we will married be.

[NELLIE starts, and turns away her head.

*Enter PRINCE NOBLEHEART in shooting costume, with a gun in his hand.
CHAMBERLAIN tries to stand between NELLIE and the PRINCE, and, in order
to hide her, draws out the flaps of his coat.*

PRINCE.

Lord Chamberlain, where's the bird I shot ?

CHAMBERLAIN *(in great agitation).*

'Tis plucked, my Prince, and in the pot.
That is to say, I've been so flurried ;
In fact, I've been so greatly hurried.
The bird you've killed, it flew away,
With *Au revoir* another day.
It was a goose—I have its feather.

PRINCE.

Birds of a feather flock together.

[Sees the PRINCESS.

What have we here beneath the shade ?
My eyes ! a stunning pretty maid !
And picking nettles—what a shame.
So this, sir, was your little game ?

CHAMBERLAIN.

She's gathering nettles, noble sir.
You nearly had made *game* of her.

PRINCE.

Her pleading eyes my heart unnerves.

CHAMBERLAIN *(aside).*

He's going to poach on my preserves.

PRINCE (*to Nellie*).

Why are you wandering here, sweet maid?

CHAMBERLAIN.

" Gathering nettles, sir," she said.

PRINCE.

She did *not* speak.

CHAMBERLAIN.

Well—yes ! 'tis rum !
I think myself the girl is dumb !

PRINCE.

What can she want with such venomous weeds ?
The tears in her blue eyes are shining like beads.
Ah ! see, she has blistered her pretty white hand.

[*Takes her hand.*

Such a heartrending object no fellow can stand.
Come forth, little maid, from the shade of the trees ;
'Tis a shame to have beauty that nobody sees.

[*Sings: " Love thee, dearest."*

Love thee dearest, love thee!
Yes, by yonder star I swear,
Which, thro' clouds above me,
Shines so brightly there.
Though too oft dim,
With tears like him,
Like him my love shall shine.
So love thee, dearest, love thee !
Yes, till death I'm thine.

My words have failed to make her speak ;
I'll plant a kiss upon her cheek.

[*Kisses her.*

CHAMBERLAIN.

That kiss my dearest hope unsettles.

[*Sits down by the wheel.*

Hallo ! I'm sitting on some nettles !

PRINCE.

Afraid of me ! Don't be so humble.

CHAMBERLAIN.

Keep her at arm's length ; she's a *dumb-bell* (e).

[NELLIE *wrings her hands.*

PRINCE.

What is it ? Eh ? the pain still lingers ?

CHAMBERLAIN.

I'm losing all patience : come, speak on your fingers.

PRINCE.

Does this silence betoken your speechless devotion ?

CHAMBERLAIN.

She does not discover the slightest emotion.

PRINCE.

I love you ! I ask you for this little hand.
Say you will be mine, and be Queen of the land.
Come, show that you love me, and give me one token.

[*He kneels ;* NELLIE *kisses him.   Exit* PRINCE *and* NELLIE.

CHAMBERLAIN (*disconsolately, with his hand on his heart*).

She doesn't care sixpence if my heart is broken.

[*Sings, to the air* "*Once I loved a maiden fair.*"

Once I loved a maiden fair,
　　But she did deceive me :
She with Venus might compare,
　　In my mind, believe me.
She was young, and among
　　All the nettles spinning :
Now I see that I was right
　　From the very beginning.

I my mind had quite made up
　　That she truly loved me ;
But she turned her nose up,
　　And thought herself above me.

Now my love I must conceal
Within this throbbing bosom ;
I must take her spinning-wheel,
And with grief pursue them.

END OF ACT III.

ACT IV.—*A Room in the Palace.*
Sound of bells and gongs, and much confusion.   Music, "Wedding Bells."
Enter CHAMBERLAIN, *with a caper.*

CHAMBERLAIN.

Such a blowing and a crowing ;
Such a coming and a going ;
Such a bowing and a scraping ;
Such a fuss and jackanaping ;
Such a brewing and a baking ;
Such ridiculous love-making ;
'Tis enough to make a fellow mad, I say.
The cause of this tumult you never could guess :
Our Prince is to marry the Silent Princess.
A Princess he calls her, but how can he tell ?
She has not, to my eyes, the air of a swell.
Her ways are too simple ; her hair is her own ;
She has neither got puffs, nor a high chignon.
Her face is not powdered ; her eyes are too bright :
I'm not often wrong, and I'm generally right.
If only she'd open her dear mouth a while,
And give us some words as sweet as her smile.
Some people might think it an excellent joke
And a very good thing if their wives never spoke.
Not so the Prince, for his pleasure it nips
To think they are silent, those sweet rosy lips.

In fact, he's a maniac; upon her he dotes,
Though from morning till night she is spinning those coats.
And——   [*Sings sentimentally, to the air of " The Organ Grinder."*
     I loved her, and she might have been
       The happiest in the land;
     But she fancied a Prince who wore a coronet
      And   diamond ring on his hand.

I certainly love her, but my temper it nettles
To see her sit down with her wheel and her nettles,
When all the great courtiers around her must stand,
And our great Prince himself in the midst of the band.
It 'll come to no good—it 'll end in a fight.
I'm not often wrong, and I'm generally right.

Enter PRINCE NOBLEHEART.

PRINCE.

Well, my Lord Chamberlain, I hope all's well.

CHAMBERLAIN.

Yes, yes, your Highness, as a marriage bell.
Her Royal Highness her apparel settles;
'Twas somewhat disarranged in gathering nettles.

PRINCE.

Nettles again! They sting me to the heart;
In this strange secret I may have no part.
Save for this mystery, I do believe
She would be loth my trusting heart to grieve;
For though some magic art her sweet voice ties,
I read her inmost thoughts within her eyes.
She has a heart as pure, yet firm of will,
As ice-bound snow upon an Alpine hill.
Go, bring her, Chamberlain; for her I pine:
The morn has come at last which makes her mine.

Summon the trumpeters—let them sound a blast :
My longed-for wedding morn has come at last.

　　　　　　　　　　　　　[Exit CHAMBERLAIN.

SONG.—*Air, " The Bridge."*

I stood in my halls at mid-day,
　　And the clock was striking the hour;
My wedding sun was shining
　　Behind the old church tower.

I felt a deep conviction
　　Within my bosom rise,
A shadow of dark affliction
　　That fell upon my eyes.

But my heart refuses sadness ;
　　The future may keep its care ;
For the present is full of gladness,
　　And I fling to the winds despair.

And for ever and for ever,
　　As long as this bosom heaves,
As long as the heart has passions,
　　As long as trees have leaves,

My love and my true affection,
　　For the girl whom I hold dear,
In every thought and action
　　Most truly shall appear.

　　　　　[Enter CHAMBERLAIN, *grinning and dancing.*

PRINCE.

How now, Lord Chamberlain, what means this grinning ?

CHAMBERLAIN.

Her Royal Highness cannot come just yet—she's spinning.

PRINCE.

Spinning !—What, spinning on her bridal morn !
Such self-imposed toil can be no longer borne.

　　　　　[Enter PRINCESS NELLIE *as a bride.*

Ah! here she comes—my sweet and blushing bride.
Come, sweetheart, hither to thy lover's side.
Hast not one word to grace our wedding day?

[NELLIE *shakes her head.*

CHAMBERLAIN.

He might as well unto a statue pray.

PRINCE.

Well, well, I'll chide thee not; all else of thine,
Except this secret, well I know is mine.
But, hark! What is it that this tumult tells?

[*Noise of tramping and shouting heard outside.*

CHAMBERLAIN.

Your Royal Highness, 'tis the wedding bells.

PRINCE.

Nay, nay, I heard a tumult in the street;
The sound of tramping horse and soldiers' feet.
Fear not, dear love, nor tremble on mine arm,
For this good sword shall shield thee from all harm.

[*Loud knocks heard.*

CHAMBERLAIN (*advancing to the door, sings*).
Who's dat knocking at de garden gate?
You cannot come in, cos you've come too late.

QUEEN SNAP-EM-UP (*at the other side of the door*).
I will come in—I will come in, I say.
An audience with Prince Nobleheart I pray.

[NELLIE *hides her face in terror.*

PRINCE.

Fear not, sweet Princess, 'tis a woman's voice:
The laws of chivalry admit no choice.
To keep a woman standing at the gate
I cannot do—e'en though it makes us late

Enter QUEEN SNAP-EM-UP.

QUEEN.

So, I have found you, traitress, in your snug retreat.
Vengeance has come with slow but certain feet.
Sire, a monster in your arms you hold,
A woman falser than can well be told.
Ask her for those six brothers whom she killed ;
Ask her for all the brothers' blood she spilled :
Six boys, with rosy cheeks and flaxen hair,
Although they wept for life, she did not spare.
Her father, broken-hearted, through his palace moans ;
He hears in every breath his children's groans.
Throughout the country there goes up one cry—
" Bring back the maiden false, that she may die."
And thou shalt die, thou maiden false as fair :
Six hundred horsemen stand upon the stair
To bear thee hence.

> [*Stretches out her hand to seize the* PRINCESS.

PRINCE.

Woman, take off thy hand !
I fear not thee, nor yet thine armèd band.
This is my bride, and I would stake my life
Upon the truth and honour of my wife.
[*To Nellie.*] Speak, dearest, speak one word in thy defence.
Her tongue is locked—her eyes speak innocence.

QUEEN.

For the base deed she wrought her tongue is tied ;
This is the proof that cannot be denied.

CHAMBERLAIN.

Speak up, young woman, put that old girl down ;
She does not look like one that owns a crown.

QUEEN.

Come, give her up to me, I must away ;
In foolish parley I'll no longer stay.

PRINCE.

Never ! for false are all the words you say.

QUEEN.

Let go of her !

PRINCE.

Again I say I won't.

QUEEN.

Then I will make you, Sire, if you don't.
[*Waves her hand over* PRINCE *and* CHAMBERLAIN, *and transfixes them.*
There for one hour you're rooted to the ground ;
And when no longer by my spell you're bound,
Look for your Princess, and you'll look in vain ;
You never more shall see her face again !
[*To Princess.*] For I'm as strong as that Witch Worthy hag,
And you resistless in these arms I'll drag
To some far prison, where in chains you'll lie
Until the hour appointed you to die.
[*Exit* PRINCESS NELLIE, *dragged out by the* QUEEN.

END OF ACT IV.

ACT V.—*Ghost music from "Faust." Turret Chamber in a Prison.*
NELLIE *alone and crying. An axe and block in the corner, and straw on the ground.*
Enter CHAMBERLAIN *cautiously, with a lantern and key in his hand.*

CHAMBERLAIN.

Some like Princes, bold and free ;
Some like Chamberlains, just like me.
Such a getting upstairs to find her in a prison,
Such a getting up stairs I never did see.

M

Hallo ! I say, I'm nearly out of breath ;
These prison stairs have almost been my death.
My eyes ! how dark and musty it is here ;
I didn't think a prison felt so queer.

                     [*Stumbles over the block.*

I must be cautious of my precious life :
My country needs me, but I need a wife.
To find this wife I've taken endless pains ;
They say the little maiden's here in chains.
I bribed the gaoler—he's a pal o' mine—
With purse of gold and flagon of good wine,
To let me in, and leave the prison key ;
And if she'll have me I will set her free.
My master thinks for him abroad I roam,
But charity, my friends, begins at home.

                     [*Sees the* PRINCESS.

Ah ! here's the Princess, crying in the dark ;
My pretty little bird, my captive lark.
Nay, shrink not, birdie, I will set you free,
I would not hurt a worm, unless it trod on me.
She's crying still, in spite of all I say.
Come, dry your eyes, and listen to me, pray.

                     [*Sits down beside her.*

I'm very fond of you, my dearest life,
And think that now perhaps you'll be my wife.

                     [*Shakes the key before her.*

Freedom is sweet ; you've but to nod your head,
And from this frightful prison you'll be led.
Come, nod your head.   [*Nellie shakes it.*]   No, that's not
     the way ;
I saw you move it right the other day.
I'm not the Prince, for he's an awful swell ;
But don't you think that I might do as well ?

I am so fond of you, you cannot think ;
I'll give you all you like to eat and drink.
I know quite well how happy you would feel.

[NELLIE *makes a sign of spinning.*]

Come, what more do you want—your spinning-wheel ?
[*Aside.*] The girl is cracked : to think at such an hour,
When I have told her that I have the power
To set her free, she needs a wheel for spinning !
I thought that she was mad from the beginning.
I'm seldom wrong ; I'm generally right.
[*To Nellie.*] Girl, do you know that you're to die to-night ?

[NELLIE *nods her head.*]

I have the key, and I can set you free :
You've only got to say you'll marry me.

[NELLIE *shakes her head.*]

Come, change your mind, I can no longer wait ;
You'll wish that I was back when 'tis too late.

[NELLIE *kneels down before him, and clasps her hands
in entreaty for the spinning-wheel.*]

CHAMBERLAIN (*impatiently*).

Bah ! of this wife who'd care to be the winner ?
She's only suited for a cotton-spinner.
Stay where you are, and soon you will be dead.
I've lost my patience ; you may lose your head.
[*Aside.*] A happy thought ! Devotion 'twould evince
To lend this key to that demented Prince.
'Twill show to him that I'm on the "*qui vive.*"
[*Aloud.*] And now, misguided girl, I'll take my leave.

[*Exit* CHAMBERLAIN.]

NELLIE *sobs herself to sleep. Ghost music from "Faust." Red fire.*

Enter WITCH WORTHY.

WITCH.

Witch Worthy gets in, despite bar and lock.
What's here in the corner ? An axe and a block !

M 2

And the poor little maid, see—she sobs in her sleep!
Such a sight would cause even my broomstick to weep.
I fear me the task cannot yet have been done.

[Takes up the coats.

But five coats are finished; the sixth is begun.
She cannot have ceased for her brothers to care,
But has left off her work in a fit of despair.
Nay! I see what it is—yes, it's clear as the day!
They have taken her wheel and her nettles away.
Ha! ha! do they think thus Witch Worthy to sell?
I'll bring them back now by a magical spell.

[Waves her wand.

One-ry, two-ery, dickery, davy:
Nettles and spinning, rise from your cavey.
Discum di, and merri-cum-ri;
Our poor little Princess must not die.

[Red fire, from the midst of which the wheel and nettles appear.

But this block in the corner speaks direst need;
She must work at her task with redoubled speed.
I'll just wake her thus, and will vanish away,
For her work will not brook of a moment's delay.

[Exit WITCH.

Ghost music from "Faust." NELLIE wakes, sees the spinning-wheel; takes it up in her arms, kisses it; sets it down again, and begins to spin. After some time Storks' voices are heard in the distance, singing:

Nell, Nell, here we are again;
Here we are again; here we are again.
Nell, Nell, here we are again:
What a jolly good mount we've made.

NELLIE starts for a moment from her wheel; looks out of the window; comes back gain and cries. PRINCE HUGH Stork puts in his head through the window bars. Chorus of Storks:

Quack! quack! here she is again! &c.
We've found little Nell at last!

PRINCE HUGH.

Come, poor little Nellie, don't cry at our quacks;
Put down that old wheel, and fly off on our backs.
Bring the block to the window, and climb by the wall;
Catch hold of our bills, and I'm sure you won't fall.

PRINCE JACK.

Come do, there's a good girl, and don't make a fuss;
Don't say you care more for the nettles than us.

[NELLIE *holds up the coats.*

PRINCE HUGH.

What's the good of these coats? My poor brain it racks.
Do you think we'll be richer for all these green backs?
Come, dear little Nellie, it cannot be true
You love us all less than we used to love you.

[NELLIE *goes on spinning.*

PRINCE JOE.

I hope you've forgiven the old days gone by;
Each one of us now for you gladly would die.
And somebody else—as you know, I dare say—
Is putting himself in a terrible way.
As we passed through the town, a little while since,
We heard of the grief of your lover, the Prince.

[NELLIE *starts and looks up from her wheel.*

PRINCE JACK.

His nerves are unstrung, and his brain is disordered;
They say his poor heart has had to be sawdered.
He's exhausted the whole of the Pharmacopœia,
And cries out each moment, "Ah, could I but see her!"
You can get through the grating—come, listen to reason;
Fly off on our backs—'tis the *migrating* season.

[*Nellie rings.*

PRINCE HUGH.

Boys! the prison bell rings, with its great iron tongue;
If you stay here much longer, your necks will be wrung.

Chorus of Storks.

Quack! quack! we'll come back to you again, &c.

Enter PRINCE NOBLEHEART *at the door.*

PRINCE.

Alack a day! how dark it's all around!
Scarce with this lamp and key my way I've found.
Ah! here she is, and at that wretched spinning;
I think this end is worse than the beginning.
Oh, dearest, speak! You must not, shall not die;
Far from this cell let us together fly.
Look at this ghastly block—this fearful axe:
The very sight of them my bosom racks.
Darling! you love me, for those eyes speak true,
And if you die—I also die with you.
But save us both. Come, let us hasten hence;
This arm and sword shall be your strong defence.

[*Tries to draw her away.* NELLIE *resists, and shows him the coats.*

[*Aside.*] Ah! much I fear that grief has turned her brain.
[*Aloud.*] Yes, yes, my child! but all this work is vain.
When you are Queen, you shall have gorgeous store
Of robes, with precious jewels broidered o'er.
And if a wish to spin you e'er should feel,
I will provide you with a golden wheel;
I will anticipate with love your needs.
But leave this dingy wheel, these stinging weeds!
Hush! I hear footsteps, and we must away;
Come, dearest, it will kill me if you stay.

[*Sings.*

I could not leave thee, though I said,
Good-bye, sweetheart, good-bye!

You will not ?—then I'll share this fate of thine.
One grave shall cover your dead heart and mine.

Enter QUEEN SNAP-EM-UP *and* EXECUTIONER.

QUEEN (*aside*).

Ah! who is this?   The Prince!   How came he here?
His hand upon his sword;—dost think I fear?
[*To the Prince.*] This is my prison—this my native land:
A thousand swords leap forth at my command.
But stay! perchance you came to see her die?
You have not long to wait—the hour is nigh!
[*To Nellie.*] Prepare for death; the clock is striking nine!
[*To Executioner.*] Off with her head!   [*To Prince.*] She is no
   longer thine.

PRINCE (*to Executioner*).

Take but one step to do thy cruel part,
I'll plunge this steel within thy recreant heart.

[*Storks' heads appear at the window.*

Quack! quack! here we are again!
To say one last farewell.

[QUEEN *starts.*

QUEEN (*aside*).

These hateful Storks!   What ill wind blows them here?
My heart forebodes that punishment is near.

Enter CHAMBERLAIN.

CHAMBERLAIN.

Birds! beasts! and fishes!   What a motley sight!
I'm not often wrong, and I'm generally right.
[*Aside.*] I thought that my master the Prince I should see,
For I gave him the lamp, and I gave him the key.
[*Aloud.*] And here's an old woman who wants to come in;
She says that she taught the young Princess to spin;
And she can explain what these mysteries mean.

QUEEN.

Executioner, hasten to finish this scene !

[*Red fire and thunder.*

Enter WITCH WORTHY.

WITCH.

Forbear ! for I have something to explain.
Queen Snap-em-up, at last we meet again !
Perhaps it is not quite a *gain* to you ;
I think this meeting you'll have cause to rue.

QUEEN.

I will not brook this interference now ;
I'll chop her head off with these hands, I vow.

[QUEEN *springs forward, and lays hold of* NELLIE. PRINCE
draws his sword. NELLIE, *having finished the last coat,
throws them at the feet of* WITCH WORTHY.

WITCH.

Sweet Princess ! are the coats of nettles spun ?
Ah, yes ! I see the noble task is done.

STORKS (*at the window*).

Nell, Nell, we cannot bear this sight ;
We cannot bear this sight ; we cannot bear this sight ;
We must say our last good-bye.

[*All look round.*

WITCH.

Now, Storks ! I stay you in your onward flight ;
Witch Worthy needs your presence here to-night.
Rest on your wings a little while below,
Whilst I on you these coats of nettles throw.
One—two—[*throws out two coats*].
[*To audience.*] What love can do.
Three—four—[*throws out two more*].
[*To audience.*] It opes the door.
Five—six—[*throws out two more*].
[*Points to the door*.] Come in, my chicks !

Triumph of Love ! Sister so firm and meek,
You've saved your brothers—now I bid you *speak!*

PRINCESS NELLIE.

Speak !   May I speak ?   And is my tongue set free ?
Prince, with my new-found voice I swear to thee
That I am innocent, though silent long,
Bearing with cruel treachery and wrong.

PRINCE.

She speaks !   Enchanting music of the spheres !
Joy of my eyes !   Now rapture of my ears !

PRINCESS NELLIE.

I loved my brothers, spite of all she said ;
They were not killed by me—they are not dead !

WITCH.

Dead !   I should think not ; though no longer birds,
On wings of love they come to prove her words.
With flying colours they are drawing near ;
Those are their footsteps on the stair we hear.

Enter six PRINCES, *marching.*

Slap ! bang ! here we are again,
To save little sister Nell.

[*Draw their swords, and close round the* QUEEN *and* EXECUTIONER.

CHAMBERLAIN.

'Tis just as I said—it would end in a fight.
I'm not often wrong, and I'm generally right.

QUEEN.

The game is lost !   This sight my soul alarms.
[*To Executioner.*] Prithee, good man, support me in thy arms.

[*Faints into the arms of* EXECUTIONER.

PRINCE.

Off with her head! Raise high the thirsting steel!
[*To Nellie.*] The doom she planned for thee, herself shall
    feel.

PRINCESS NELLIE.

Mercy, great Prince! if that you love me well,
And that you love me needs no words to tell.
Spare this poor Queen—thy hasty order stay.
Oh! let no harsh deed mar this happy day.
Forgive her, as I do, and set her free;
And, brothers, sheathe your swords, for love of me.

PRINCE.

That long-lost voice my heart cannot withstand.
You are my Queen—I bow to your command.

PRINCE HUGH.

You've saved us, Nellie; we'll do what you please.
But you, old "Snap-up," down upon your knees,
And beg her pardon for your shameful lies.
You shall not stir until she bids you rise.

> [*Forces her down on her knees.*

QUEEN.

Forgive me, Nellie, ere my reign I close,
And never in this land I'll show my nose.

> [NELLIE *raises the* QUEEN.

PRINCESS NELLIE.

Here is my hand! Let all this rancour cease.

CHAMBERLAIN.

High rank or humble, we are all at peace:
And while of peace we have a little chance,
Let's all take hands and have a break-down dance.

[PRINCES *sheathe their swords, and form a line at the back of the stage.
The chief actors form a line in front. The* PRINCE, *standing a
little more forward than the rest, sings the following song to the
air "Polly Perkins." All join in the chorus of each verse, take
hands and dance.*

There was an old Queen Snap-em-up, so grewsome and grand ;
So bold and so bilious she ruled in the land.
Oh, she famished us and she damaged us, and spoilt all our joys,
And made very ugly fowls of six dear little boys.
    [*Chorus.*] Oh, she famished us, &c.

Oh ! there was an old Lord Chamberlain, so tall and so spruce,
Who thought himself a swell, but who was an old goose ;
For he goggled it and he boggled it—his legs were so long ;
And always he ended being generally wrong.
    [*Chorus.*] For he goggled it, &c.

There was a little womany, whose broom was of switch,
A dear little crickety enchanting old witch ;
For she made it her business to set everything right,
And she hopes for an intimation she bewitched you to-night.
    [*Chorus.*] For she made it her business, &c.

There were six jolly Princes who were changed into Storks,
Had to gobble with long mandibles, instead of knives and forks.
Oh ! they clattered it and they spattered it, with a hop and a
    splash,
And moulted their plumage with a mild nettle rash.
    [*Chorus.*] Oh ! they clattered it, &c.

There was a pretty Princess, so gentle and young,
Who saved a whole young family by holding her tongue ;
So winning at her spinning at the coats of green leaves,
While her poor little feathered relatives picked their wings on the
    eaves.
    [*Chorus.*] So winning at her spinning, &c.

There was a young lover who, the Prince Nobleheart plays,
But who finds himself too modest to sing his own praise ;
For his gallantry and 'his courtesy, and his heart stout and true,
If there's any pretty observation, he leaves it to you.

    [*Chorus.*] For his gallantry, &c.

        [*Red fire.*   WITCH *advances to the front of the stage.*

WITCH.

All's well that ends well.   Do I hear you say,
" No longer now exists a witch or fay ;
They are old fables of a bygone time ? "
There's moral hidden in *our* fairy rhyme.
While love and courage still may play their part,
There lingers something of the witch's art ;
And if your loud applause this truth denotes,
Pray come another night to see our " Nettle Coats."

        [*Curtain falls.*

THE END.

LONDON : R. OLAY, SONS, AND TAYLOR, BREAD STREET HILL.

www.ingramcontent.com/pod-product-compliance
Lightning Source LLC
Chambersburg PA
CBHW031114020726
47495CB00007B/2188